A SEASON FOR BLISS

A SEASON FOR BLISS

Other Books By Jacki Kelly

THE SWEET ROAD SERIES

The Sweet Road Home
The Sweet Road To Love
The Sweet Road Back

DATING JUST GOT SERIOUS

Blind Date
One Date At A Time
Date Me
A Single Date
Speed Date
Dating Just Got Serious – Box Set
Done With Dating

THE BAPTISTE SERIES

Packed and Ready To Go
Going Backwards

JOIN THE JACKI KELLY NEWSLETTER at

http://jackikelly.com

and get a free book.

You'll be able to stay tuned to new releases, appearances, events and prizes. She's always giving something away.

Chapter One

Bliss Duncan stood on the Penn Station platform, huddled with a swarm of happy passengers waiting to board the train to all points south for the Christmas holidays. From the bubbling conversations and the massive smiles on the other traveler's faces, she had to be the only one not overjoyed about making the trip. Family gatherings zapped her energy, the questions about her life, the snide remarks about her answers, the pressure to be perfect. Just thinking about what was to come left her drained and inert. But her mother had insisted she come home early for the holidays and, like any good daughter, she obeyed.

Her phone vibrated in her hand. She glanced at the screen before accepting the call from Keith. He was turning out to be way too needy for someone who didn't know how to reciprocate.

"What's up, Keith?" She tried not to sigh into the phone.

"You sound like I'm bothering you."

"I'm getting ready to board the train, so I won't be able to talk long. You should have just come home with me for the holidays. My family is cool, they don't bite."

"I need some time to think. This thing at work has me up-against-the-wall. They're looking at me like I'm some kind of cannibal. I would never put people's lives in danger. They have to know I'm not the one who falsified those records."

"Breathe, Keith. You just need to get out of bed, get dressed, and try to live a normal life until this is all over." She pushed ahead as the crowd began to move. "Once you talk to the investigators and show your documentation, then everything is going to be fine."

"But you should be here with me. What kind of girlfriend leaves her man in the middle of a crisis?"

She rolled her eyes towards the ceiling. Coddling him through this eruption in his life was like taking care of an infant. He whined and fussed non-stop. The constant moping around was dragging her under right along with him. If he'd been a more nurturing boyfriend then maybe she wouldn't have minded, but before this scandal broke he'd all but ignored her most of the time. Their relationship was on life support and she was ready to pull the plug.

"I've had this trip planned for months. You knew I had to come home. I missed Thanksgiving with my family and my mother would have a mega-melt-down if I tried to blow them off for Christmas. Besides, I think we need a little space right now."

"I told you Megan was a mistake. You spend so much time in the office I just needed someone to talk to. And all we did was talk."

"All you did was take something bad and make it worse."

The phone went dead. "He hung up on me again." She stared at the dark screen before shoving it into her purse. "Big, baby," she muttered.

Keith's microwave mentality was as childish as he was. The moment the world stopped revolving around him, he thought the sky was falling.

She boarded the train and found a seat. The train jerked away from the platform. Within moments the rhythmic sound of steel and metal lulled her into a sense of foreboding that wouldn't let go. This was not the time to let her foot off the throttle at work. While Keith's career might be swirling down the drain, her prospects were bright for a change. One slip-up or missed detail and everything she'd worked so hard for could be yanked away.

The two-hour ride gave her time to catch up on phone messages and work on the year-end status report before slapping on her happy face and pretending to be ecstatic about being home for the Christmas holidays. And the break away from Keith gave her plenty of time to think about their relationship. Which is more than he'd done in the last year. He was sulking again about something she had done or hadn't done. Either way, there was more bickering to come. He didn't understand her need to work so hard. Her ambition was a personal affront to his laid back, don't care attitude. But she wouldn't let his attitude about work impact her.

Bliss looked at the battery icon on her phone and her heart double-stepped. "Oh damn, my battery is dying." Bliss dropped the phone on the pull down tray next to her lap-top.

The gentleman seated beside her leaned over the armrest just enough to encroach into her space. "Is something wrong?"

She'd barely noticed him when she stepped on the train and took her seat. But she should have. His salt and pepper hair was just as striking as his facial features.

If she'd had something other than work on her mind, she would have been talking to him long before now. Making friendly conversation with a handsome stranger on a train ride home was in no way comparable to what Keith had done. It didn't even come close to what he'd done with Megan. "No, nothing's wrong. My cell phone battery is dying. I don't think it's going to last until I get off." She dug in her purse. "My charger should be in here. I packed in such a hurry I was throwing stuff everywhere."

"Maybe that's for the best. This is the quiet car." He pointed at the sign posted over the door. His calming baritone voice erased the sting of the reprimand. "And I can't imagine you can find anything in that huge purse."

"Thank you." She gave him one of her stony looks, one that she preserved just for Keith when he was being a major pain in-the-you-know-where.

She stole another glance at the gentleman seated next to her. A thick book rested in his lap as he turned the page. His fingers were long with neatly manicured nails. She couldn't help but wonder if anything else about him was as long and intriguing.

She pointed at him. "You look familiar." She shifted in her seat to get a better look. "University of Delaware. Introduction to Marketing. You were the Assistant Professor. Dr. Winbush."

He studied her for a moment. "And if my memory doesn't fail me, you're the young lady who sat in the last row texting during my lectures. I remember the face, even though your curls covered most of your face, but not the name." His smile was even, accentuating his dimples.

"Bliss Duncan. And please don't judge me too hard. I was young. A Sophomore. I didn't know any better. Are you still at the University?"

"No. It didn't take me long to realize academia wasn't for me."

"Do you know how many times the women in your classes tried to get your attention? I'm not talking about for academic reasons either."

"I heard the whispers. But students were off limits."

"You look different." He was much more handsome now, the gray on his temples made him look distinguished, well traveled.

"I grayed early. It's hereditary."

"I think the gray makes you even more distinguished. If that's at all possible." She pushed away the naughty thoughts crowding for attention in her head. She directed her gaze back into her own space. If Keith hadn't been mad at her for the last week, she wouldn't be horny and admiring long ago crushes on a train.

The ping from her phone signaled an incoming text message. She picked it up and glanced at the screen. The message was from Keith. With one hand poised over the computer keyboard, she used her other hand to scroll through his message.

'This just isn't going to work. If you can't be here for me when I need you, then maybe I don't need you. Let's take a break. A long one. You're too busy for a boyfriend. You have your precious job and your family. Good-bye Bliss.'

"He broke up with me. I can't believe he broke up with me." She blurted. With the phone still clenched in her hand, she held it up for him to see, as if she needed a witness to her humiliation. "Who breaks up with someone by sending a text message? Keith is such a jerk." Her voice was edged with the kind of disappointment she'd become too familiar with. If Keith had been nearby, she would have clocked him with the cell phone.

Dr. Winbush nodded like he thought the outburst was ordinary from random passengers on a train. He sat up straighter. She was happy to have his full attention now. "If your boyfriend breaks up with you in such a callous way, he wasn't worth your time" He paused. "You're obviously a beautiful woman and based on how you've been pounding on that computer since you sat down, you're accomplished. You don't need him. It's his loss." He shrugged a shoulder as if he'd solved all of her problems with his quick synopsis.

She clutched the phone to her chest. "He said I was so busy I didn't need a boyfriend." She swallowed. "I'm trying to get a promotion. Living in Manhattan is expensive. If he wasn't such an underachiever and hadn't drawn suspicion on his questionable business practices, he wouldn't be in this predicament. Christmas is two days away. He probably just didn't want to buy me a gift. He's so cheap, he could be a free sample."

"Based on your activity for the few minutes we've been on the train, he might have a justifiable gripe." He glanced at his watch. "You've barely looked up from your computer since you sat down, except for the few glances you've given me—once you noticed I was sitting next to you."

"You noticed that, huh? I was trying to be discreet."

"Then you're not very good at it. I wish I could have had that kind of attention from you when you were in my class." The knowing smile he gave her said he was teasing.

She tucked her hair back to turn her full attention on him. "I did get an A in the class."

"You can call me Marc, and you probably should have only gotten a B. I was being generous. Since you attended all of my study sessions, I gave you an A for trying."

"I probably shouldn't admit this, but do you know I used to follow you around campus?"

"I did not know that. I thought us running into each other was only coincidence."

"I was pretty stealthy back then. I don't know if I could be that discrete now."

"Now you don't need to be." His voice dropped an octave. The words sounded like an invitation. One she wanted to accept.

She directed her attention back to her computer. "This report is due on my manager's desk right after the holidays. If my parents hadn't demanded I come home early, I would have finished it before leaving the city." She spoke with the indignation she always used when being judged. "No one ever tells men they work too hard."

"I'm sure you have a good reason. Everyone who works nonstop thinks they do. I used to think getting the syllabus out on time and preparing for the next exam were the most important things in the world, so I understand. You're young. A millennial. Right now, you think your job is your life. You were willing to put your boyfriend on the back burner for it as if he was always going to be there. Kinda like leftovers."

She drew back to get a good look at him. He'd used his wisdom to point out what he thought were her shortcomings as if his age gave him a free pass to judge her. He wasn't as old as her father, but he sure was acting like him.

She studied him for a moment, trying to determine his age. The salt and pepper hair made it impossible.

"I'm forty. In case you want to know."

"I didn't...I mean I would never ask," she said.

"I don't mind saying my age. For me, it's just a number."

"I see. Well, look, Marc. I'm sure your words of wisdom would work for someone else, but you don't know my situation. I was passed over last year for a promotion. I was told I need to prove myself. Women are always told that. Were you ever told you needed to prove yourself before you could be given a job? Of course not." She stopped long enough to take a breath. "No, men are given the job first. I actually had to train my manager on how to use the marketing software. And now he wants me to prove I can handle a job I know inside and out. I just think that's code for sit back and wait until we think you're worthy of the promotion. Well, I'm tired of waiting. Next year is my year." She gathered her hair at the nape of her neck.

"I never said you didn't have a valid reason for ignoring your boyfriend. But you have to be ready to accept the consequences of what happens when you ignore people you care about." Marc kept his nicely manicured hands in his lap.

"Look...I shouldn't have dropped my problems on your shoulders. It's not like Keith and I had some great relationship. If he hadn't broken it off, I probably would have cut him loose as soon as I got the time. We haven't been vibing lately. But at least I would have told him to his face. Because that's the kind of person I am."

"A notable quality. Then you should consider his deed a gift. An early Christmas present."

She turned in her seat and settled against the soft cushion. High maintenance. That's what Keith had called her. Spitting the words out like they coated his mouth with something foul. Being busy at work served as a convenient distraction for avoiding the inevitable. Now that the finality of their relationship was sitting on her phone, she waited for the unhappiness to arrive. The part of her that was supposed to be sad at being dumped just before the holidays.

Nothing.

Absolutely nothing, and she'd been dumped often enough to know the feeling. Instead, a heady excitement rushed her stomach.

She faced Marc. "You know, I'm not sad. I don't think I even care that he broke up with me." There was no hitch in her voice. She hoped she didn't sound callous. "That's just one less thing I'll have to worry about over the holidays." At least it was all true.

"It worked out for the both of you then. A silver lining." Marc had a remarkable smile. One she'd continued to remember long after they parted ways.

The conductor announced the Wilmington stop. Bliss shoved her computer into her messenger bag and her phone into her purse.

"This is my stop." She glanced at Marc. "Thank you for allowing me to vent. Enjoy your holidays." She stood to move past him.

"I'm getting off too." He reached overhead to remove a duffel bag from the bin. "You're a Delawarean?"

"Born and raised just outside of Wilmington. How about you?"

He stepped aside and allowed her to exit the train in front of him. "No. I'm originally from Virginia. My wife was from Delaware."

Bliss stepped off the train onto the platform. The frigid air pierced her wool coat. She pulled her cashmere gloves from her pocket and slipped them on. The temperature felt ten degrees colder than when she'd boarded the train. The wind on the platform whipped her scarf loose from her coat.

Marc caught it. "I think you had better secure this tighter if you plan to hold on to it."

She accepted the pink and green scarf and tied it around her neck twice. After thanking him, she descended the stairs into the warmth of the station. All she wanted to do was get home, pull off her heels and curl up in the full-size bed she grew up in. Not because she wanted to cry or commiserate about her break-up. Being alone for just a few moments sounded like a treat she deserved.

She stepped out of the station along with twenty other passengers. At least Marc was nowhere in sight, so the one witness to her humiliation had evaporated into the night. She could spin the break-up any way she wanted. Her version wouldn't include a phone and she'd be the one making the break-up announcement.

At the intersection, there was no sign of her parent's car. She walked in the opposite direction, beyond the dwindling line of taxis. She fished her phone from her purse, hoping for just enough battery power to make one more call. The screen was black. She tightened the scarf around her neck and hunched her shoulders forward to keep the wind out.

"Need a lift?" She turned to see Marc standing behind her. Why couldn't she stop melting every time she heard his velvet voice?

"My father is supposed to pick me up." She pushed her coat sleeve up to glance at her watch. "He should be here any minute. If not I can always catch a cab."

"I don't think a cab is going to be an option." He pointed over his shoulder. "They're all gone. It's a holiday weekend, remember?"

"I talked to my father just before I boarded the train. I'm sure he didn't forget. Do you have a phone I can use to call him?" She shuffled from one foot to the other to stay warm.

He reached into the breast pocket of his coat and removed his cell. "Sure."

She dialed the home number. After several rings, there was no answer. "Let me dial his cell." She punched in the numbers without waiting for Marc to respond.

"Dad, I'm at the station. Where are you?"

"At the hospital."

#####

Marc studied Bliss' features. She had the kind of beauty that everyone noticed, both men and women. Not the kind found at cosmetic counters or in expensive potions, but the kind of beauty one is born with. Her flawless skin gleamed in the soft lights shining from the main entrance of the train station. Even though her lipstick had all been chewed away, there was still a rosy hue to her mouth. She had been the prettiest woman in his marketing class that first year he taught. He remembered her well. Long legs, long dark hair, and eyes he wanted to get lost in.

At the pace she was pushing herself, she'd have fine lines in her forehead and around her mouth before her thirtieth birthday. Nobody knew better than him what kind of havoc stress wrecked on a body. The last few years of his life, he'd lived with the devastation. The nightmarish dreams still spun him out of a sound sleep, leaving his shaking body chilled and wrung out like a dish towel.

She was him, ten years removed. Trying to keep up with the rat race before he realized the pace was ten times faster than he could ever be. But she was young and probably thought she would never grow old and tired and weary.

She ended the call and handed it to him. "My father is at the hospital. It's my mother." She didn't blink. "Can you--"

"Of course I can give you a lift. Is everything okay?" He pointed across the street. "My car is in the parking garage."

"She's at Christiana Hospital...she had a very bad fall...he sounds worried...maybe...what." She stumbled over her words. Her professional exterior wavering with each step, replaced by vulnerability, something he hadn't expected to see from her earlier professional facade.

He placed his hand at her elbow and guided her across the street. "I'm so sorry. Let me carry your bag." He led her toward the Prius, unlocking the car with the keyfob. She sat in the seat without pulling her legs inside. Her large eyes looked even bigger. Lined with a hopelessness that made him ache to hold her. She pulled her legs inside and turned in the seat. He closed the door, placed her bags in the trunk and then ran around to the driver's side.

"Do you have a charger? I need to make my phone useful." Her voice wobbled.

"Sure." He opened the glove compartment, removed the charger, then turned the ignition key. The sound of Christmas music filled the car.

"I thought I packed my charger in my bag. I was so rushed and this bag is so full of useless stuff, I may have forgotten it. So, if I'm stuck in Wilmington for several days, I'm going to have to buy a new one." She removed a tissue from her purse.

She blew her nose before pulling another tissue from the pack and dabbed her eyes. "I like the music. You're in the Christmas spirit." Her face was pinched. "Can we turn the music down a little? I need to make a few calls."

He lowered the volume, then backed out of the slot and made his way to the exit. "You're not going to call your boyfriend are you?"

She rubbed her thumb over the phone. "I was going to call my brother to see if he knows anything. But why shouldn't I call Keith? I have a few choice words I'd like to serve up for him."

"The sap broke up with you in a text message, days before Christmas. Let him stew for a few days. You've got to make him think you really don't care. Besides, he's probably too angry right now to hear your selection of words." He merged onto the highway heading south. "I know you might find this hard to believe, but men hate being ignored as much as women do. We just keep it to ourselves."

She nodded. Her thick mane of dark curls fell across her face. "Can you drive faster?" She twisted the tissue around her finger.

"I could if I wanted to get pulled over. There is a police car right behind me."

She glanced over the seat then turned back around. "Sorry. I guess I just want to hurry up and get there. My mother is never sick. For her to go to the hospital during the holidays means she must be pretty bad. She starts preparing for Christmas the day after Thanksgiving. I imagine by now she's got the Christmas tree up, all the presents wrapped, lights strung from one end of the house to the other, and the turkey ready to pop in the oven."

"Sounds wonderful."

"It isn't." She shook her head. "Mom thinks everything stops for Christmas. She believes if a miracle is going to happen, then Christmas is the appointed time. She swears that's when the angels and all the holy deities will descend from the heavens and touch the gifted individuals. She called me three times last week, demanding I come home earlier than usual, even though I tried to tell her I had a major report due. I wanted to get it done before I left the city. But she was relentless."

"Maybe she wanted you to come early because she wasn't feeling well."

She made a small sound before clutching the scarf draped around her throat. The color in her cheeks was gone.

"I'm sure your mother just wants to enjoy your company." He didn't mean to upset her. She looked as vulnerable as a kitten sitting in the middle of a highway.

"That's the same thing my father said when I tried to push back. I'm on the fast track at work. This is not the time for me to slack off. Companies don't want women that are into holidays and having babies or getting married for that matter. I've heard the men in my office whispering about the women." She twisted the tissue around her index finger, pulling so hard it snapped into two pieces.

"It sounds like you work with a bunch of jerks. All companies are not like that."

"Probably more than you think."

He pulled up to the main entrance of the hospital and stopped. She reached for the door handle. This was the perfect time to let her go and move on with his mundane life. The life that had chosen him when Rachel died. But he was tired of being dead on the inside. Everyone said he'd get back to normal one day, but he'd never believed them until now. Talking to Bliss was the most enjoyment he'd had in years. Just talking with her had awakened the man in him that longed for company and companionship.

"Wait a minute. I have your bags in the trunk. I don't expect you to lug them around inside." He glanced past her into the stark lights of the big building. "Tell me your mother's name. I'll park and come in to find you."

Her brows drew close together as if she hadn't comprehended his words.

"Your mother's name, what is it?"

"April Duncan," she said with the blank cast still on her face.

Before he could reassure her, she disappeared inside the revolving door.

Finding a parking space was easy. The late hour and close proximity to Christmas must have discouraged the masses from being sick or diminished their enthusiasm to do something about it.

He jumped out of the car like a man with a woman on his mind. Bliss had touched his deadened senses. Within minutes, he made his way through the same door Bliss had gone through and to the information desk.

With her mother's information scribbled on a piece of paper, he walked to the bank of elevators.

When he'd left New York earlier that afternoon, he'd had his whole evening mapped out. Dinner from his favorite take-out joint, some music, and maybe a little reading before going to bed. So how did he end up here? The last place on earth he would think to be. The smell was the same, and if the hospital had a taste it would be dirt. He leaned against the elevator wall until the car came to a stop.

After several deep breaths, the wave of sickness subsided. He took his time drawing in air until his lungs began to burn before releasing the breath through his mouth. By now this place should have been purged from his system, but the pain still rattled around in his bones like a ghost with no place to rest.

From his position in the hall, he glanced toward the bay of rooms where Bliss' mother should have been. He spotted Bliss coming out of a room with a tall, older gentlemen. Her father, no doubt. The somber expression on their faces was like watching a painful tableau of his past. This time, instead of him, the image had been replaced by a becoming woman who was too young to know pain. When the father disappeared through the door, she wiped her eyes before looking up.

Unsure if he should turn away to give her privacy or proceed toward her, she erased his doubt when she waved to him.

"Do you know anything? How is she?"

She shook her head. "They're running tests. She's got a broken ankle and a sprained wrist, her blood pressure is dangerously low, and they're pumping her with fluids to get it up. Since she blacked out before the fall, it could be something serious." Her words came out in a halting fashion as if speaking was new to her. "I can't believe this. I talked to her the other day and she sounded perfect. She was going on and on about the holidays and all the stuff she had to do." Her bottom lip trembled. He led her to the waiting area.

This was not the bargain he made with the gods when he woke up this morning. Hospitals were always full of gloom and sadness, and already he'd broken his vow of never returning here unless he was unconscious. But what choice did he have? He couldn't have abandoned Bliss in the cold in front of the train station any more than he could have

abandoned Rachel as she wasted away into the wife
he hardly recognized but couldn't stop loving.

Chapter Two

Bliss settled into the chair. Sobs tore through her like a hurricane in warm water. Her whole body shook. Her mother didn't look like a woman who had just fallen. Bliss's imagination filled in the blanks that the doctors couldn't until the test results came back. Each health possibility she came up with was worse than the one before.

This couldn't be happening. Maybe if her mother had complained of an ache or a pain, then the shock of being in the hospital before Christmas with such grim news wouldn't have been as devastating. But the look on her father's face and the way he spoke with uncertainty had clobbered her.

The only person to console her was Marc, who thought she didn't know how to live her life. By now, he had to be convinced she was a lunatic. Marc fed her fresh tissues as she discarded one after another with tears that didn't seem to have an end.

"I'm sorry to drag you into this." She sniffed. "I should have had you bring my bags in, then you could be on your way. As soon as my brother gets here, he'll help me."

Marc patted her arm. "This isn't a problem. I wish there was something I could do to help you."

He sounded sincere. She tried to push her lips up into something she hoped resembled a smile, but her mouth failed to cooperate. She slouched back in the chair. If Joshua didn't get here soon, she'd retrieve her bags and set Marc free. There was something in his body language that said he'd rather be somewhere else.

Her father entered the waiting room and made his way toward her. He took the empty seat next to her. Sandwiched between her father and Marc, she felt small but protected.

Marc stuck out his hand. "Hello, I'm Marc Winbush."

Her father nodded. "Clark Duncan. I owe you thanks for bringing Bliss to the hospital. I tried to reach her before...but all I got was voice mail." His voice was strained. He was more upset than he appeared.

Bliss used the tissue Marc handed her to wipe her nose.

"Honey, pull yourself together. No matter what happens, you are going to need to be strong. On the way to the hospital, your mother made me promise to keep our holiday tradition. In all the years we've been together I have never broken a promise to that woman. I'm not about to start now."

"If the two of you need some privacy..." Marc stood. The wide cast to his stance said he wanted to put as much distance between her and this depressing situation as quickly as possible.

"No, not at all." Her father motioned Marc to return to his seat.

"I should have known something was going on with your mother. She was dragging around the house like she was shackled. You know by now she would have had everything in place." He studied his massive hands, rubbing them together like he always did when he was searching for the right words. "I thought she was waiting for you to come home so the two of you could do everything together." He dropped his head and rubbed the bald spot that seemed to grow wider every time Bliss saw him. "You're going to have to do this, Bliss."

"Do what?" She recoiled away from him and landed against Marc's chest.

"Make this holiday your mother wants," his voice was barely audible.

"I can't—." She shook her head in rapid succession. "I can't."

"You have to. If we want your mom to get well, we have to make sure she's not worrying about us. You know how she is. Remember that time she had the flu and she wouldn't go to bed until I made that big pot of soup? We have to make an effort. Fiona has been there for all of us and we're going to do this thing no matter what. Do you hear me?" His voice was stronger now. He was back to giving orders, sounding like the father she grew up with and couldn't wait to get away from.

"What difference will it make if she's not there to see it? How can we celebrate when we don't even know what is wrong with her?"

"It will make a difference to her." He sat up straighter as if the more he thought about the idea the more he was invested in his plan. If the belief that blazed in his eyes was any indicator, then her mother was going to pull through based on his pure determination. "When she asks me, I can look her in the face and tell her we're doing what she asked. It won't be a lie. Do you understand?"

Maybe her head was clouded, but her father's proposal sounded ridiculous. She shook her head. This couldn't be happening. None of it. She was supposed to come home, finish her reports, and enjoy the slower pace for her parents' sake. Now her mother was sick, Keith broke up with her, and she was in the hospital with a man she hardly even knew. A man she used to follow around campus daydreaming about. While everyone else was connecting the dots, she couldn't follow the logic in the situation.

"Bliss, are you listening to me? We can do this for your mother and we will." His voice was stronger for the first time since sitting down. He pulled a piece of paper from his pants pocket. "This is a list of the gifts she put in your bedroom and who they are for. You'll need to wrap them like your mother would. You'll need to buy a Christmas tree. The decorations are in the basement in the same place as always. And you'll need to cook the Christmas Eve family dinner. All the usual stuff that your mom always prepares, the Christmas Eve dinner, wrapping the gifts, decorating the tree. If your mother could pull this off every year, you and Joshua can do it." He pushed the piece of paper into her hand.

Bliss fell back against the seat. Her heart couldn't keep up with her breaths. She was wasting time by protesting. She always did what her parents wanted, so this wasn't the time to pretend things would be any different. "Okay. I'll do my best. But you and I both know that Joshua is useless."

Her father locked eyes with her. The torment she saw on his face ripped through her like a razor. He needed this too. He was no more ready to let go of her mother's traditions than she was. But at least she had a life to go back to—well almost—but if her mother didn't make it, her father would be stuck in the remnants of whatever her mother had left behind.

"Joshua is about as dependable as a bird. He'll promise me everything and do nothing." Exhaustion hung to her words. "There is no way I can do it the way mom did--or even come close—but I'll do my best."

He gathered her in his arms and squeezed so tight she squirmed loose. "No use hanging out here. Go home and get started. As soon as I see the doctor or hear something, I'll call you."

He walked out of the room. There was a new hunch to his shoulders. His heavy footsteps scuffed the linoleum floor.

"I don't believe this. How am I supposed to do all the things he just mentioned? There isn't enough time and I can't cook a decent Christmas meal. My specialty is frozen chicken fingers that I stick in the oven. I haven't decorated a tree in years. Okay, when I was little I hung a few ornaments on the tree, but my mother always had to go back and rearrange them. And what about my report? If I don't get it submitted on time, I can start waving goodbye to my promotion."

"Slow down." Marc patted her arm, with calming strokes. "If your mother could do all this stuff, then you can do it too. If you thought all this stuff," He pointed to the piece of paper in her hand, "would make your mom better, wouldn't you jump at the chance to do everything?"

"Yeah, but—"

"Then that's your answer. You don't have to do it as good as she did. You just have to at least try. Make the effort and as you are checking things off the list, think about your mother and how happy she will be."

She stared at him. Why was she listening to this man? He was as close to a stranger as the family sitting several rows away. He didn't know anything about her or her family. Of course, he'd think it was easy. Watching was always easier than doing. In a few minutes, he would go skipping back to his perfect life and she'd probably never see him again.

"I'll help." His face was inches from hers, crowding the restricted space she marked as sacred.

"Why? Why would you want to help me? You don't really know me. One class and a few study sessions don't count. I'm sure your family has stuff they want you to do."

"Look, this isn't about me right now. Let me help. Besides I've spent the last four hours with you. I know more about you than I know about most women I date. I've even met your father."

"And you've seen my ugly cry face." She tried to laugh.

"I don't know. I didn't think it was ugly at all, in fact, far from it," he said with a small grin.

Marc walked Bliss to the front door of the modest home on Bissell Lane. The ride to her parents' house did her good. She'd stopped crying and seemed to be more relaxed. He couldn't help snatching quick glances at her. She was stunning. Much prettier than he'd remembered. He hadn't been drawn to a woman in five years, but the warmth running through his veins was very familiar. Every lustful organ in his body vibrated with new life, new desires.

He took a deep breath of the cold night air, thankful they were no longer sitting in the waiting area in the hospital. The smell of sickness and death and neglect no longer clung to the fine hairs in his nostrils. Of course the timing was wrong, but patience was something he had plenty of. Five years alone proved that.

He placed her bags just inside the door. The only thing stronger than the compulsion to kiss her was the compulsion to get far away from her. He wasn't ready to get entangled in a liaison even if the temptress was golden and gorgeous. For the first time since Rachel's death, the holidays had a real purpose. This was an opportunity to have a Christmas like the ones he used to have before Rachel got sick. The idea bloomed in his heart like a new beginning.

"I really don't think saying thank you is enough based on everything you've done for me today. I guess you never knew talking to a stranger on the train could get you involved in so much family drama. Now you know why parents tell their children not to talk to strangers."

"It was nothing. I think I was where I needed to be." He straightened and shoved his hands into his pockets. Her eyes were riveted on him, revealing her tears were replaced with worry. She hadn't stopped fidgeting since they pulled out of the hospital parking lot. He removed his coat and placed it on the chair by the door. "Now show me where the Christmas stuff is and I'll bring it up."

She dropped her coat on top of his. "I'll help you."

She led the way down a wide hall before opening the door to the basement. A single low wattage bulb lit the stairs to the cold space. Clutter was stacked in every corner of the large room. These time capsules of her family's memories reminded him of his own basement. All of Rachel's things that he hadn't given away were tucked into boxes as if she might come back one day to reclaim them.

"There." She pointed to three big cardboard boxes with the word 'Christmas' scrawled across the side. He gazed at the collection without moving.

"Is something wrong?"

"I just...I just..." She drew a breath. "Let's just get this over with." She reached for a box and hoisted it against her chest. Then she turned toward the stairs.

He grabbed the nearest box and followed her. "Where do you guys usually put your tree?"

"In the living room, right in front of this window." She put the box down and opened the lid.

"I'll go get the other one. I'll be right back."

By the time he returned, she'd scattered the contents of her box across the floor. Festive red and gold ornaments took up the space around her. "Suppose she doesn't make it?" Bliss stared at the Christmas decorations without focusing.

Her pain was visible. He'd seen anguish like that before. He'd felt it. There was no escaping the vile way it took over your body and made you doubt everything. Even your name.

"You've got to keep positive thoughts." Hadn't someone said that to him? Back then the statement had made sense, it wasn't until Rachel died that he realized how empty the words were. Just one of those empty phrases people say when they can't think of anything else. "Get some rest and I'll pick you up first thing in the morning. You've got a long list of stuff to do."

"No. I don't expect you to help me with my father's crazy idea. My brother should be arriving first thing in the morning and together we'll get..."

"You don't sound very hopeful."

"You don't know my brother. He's not very dependable." She stood and turned on the light in the adjoining dining room. She should have been exhausted, but she looked as fresh as she did when she boarded the train, except for the smear of mascara under her eyes.

Years ago, when Rachel got sick, she faded away a little each day. One morning he woke up and the vibrant woman he'd married was gone. That's when he learned to stop expecting anything from life.

Each moment was a gift, and as long as he expected nothing, he wasn't disappointed. But in the harsh light of the Duncan home, that philosophy seemed ill-placed.

Bliss had a magnetic pull that surrounded him and hadn't let go. She stirred up sentiment he'd given up on a long time ago. The house was too big for her to rattle around in thinking about what might happen to her mother.

"I should offer you something to drink. I'm sure my parents have a beer or something. Come on." Without waiting for him to reply, she made her way through the house, turning on lights along the way. The kitchen was unexpectedly modern compared to the rest of the house. She removed two bottles of beer from the refrigerator.

"I can never unscrew the caps—do you mind?" She held the bottles out to him.

He opened both beers, then sat at the kitchen counter next to her, before sliding one of the bottles toward her. "You've told me you've got a demanding job in Manhattan. Does that mean you got your degree or did your phone hinder your studies?"

"Mr. Smarty-Pants, I graduated with honors. After your class, I got more serious about school."

"After my class?"

"Yeah, there were no more good-looking professors to distract me." A wicked smile lit up her face. She was flirting and her effort stirred in his heart. Was she trying to make an old guy feel good, or did she think flattery was suitable payment for his efforts today?

"Oh, I see." He nestled his chin in his palm. "Then my leaving saved your college education."

"Yes. That's one way to look at it. I was always serious about school, but I can get distracted pretty easily. I think that's a habit I've broken."

"Good to know. Maybe while you're home for the holidays, I can take you out."

She perked up. "A date. You mean I could call all my friends and tell them I'm going out with Professor Winbush?"

"I'm not a professor anymore. I'm just Marc. I'm sure your friends will think you're crazy to be dating someone this much older." He ran his finger through his gray temples. "This gray hair is not a turn on for all women."

"Don't be so sure. I think it gives you that suave, debonair appeal."

He stood. "I better get going. You've had...you've had quite a day. And your brain is fuzzy."

Her face dropped.

"I'll tell you what. We can go Christmas tree shopping together in the morning. What time should I be here? I need a Christmas tree too, so we might as well shop together." It was a lie. He hadn't bought a tree, decorated a tree or even cared about a tree in five years. Something unfamiliar was going on. Later, during the long hours when sleep eluded him, he'd figure out what was happening, but for now the warmth in his veins was enjoyable. For a few moments, he allowed the feeling to envelop him.

Chapter Three

In the morning, Bliss sat up in bed in a room where she'd spent most of her childhood. How many years had it been since she'd spent any real time in the room? A day here or there, but this might be an extended visit if her mother didn't get home soon.

There weren't many changes from the way she'd left the room when she started living on campus. Would her parents keep the time capsule long after she established her own life with a husband and kids? Or maybe they thought she'd never have the typical family, only a series of boyfriends that would pass in and out of her life, that's why they kept this room the same, so she'd have a soft place to land.

On the far bedroom wall, the large red arrows she'd painted were still there. Back then, she'd been thrilled that her parents had allowed her to showcase her creativity. But now she could see the crooked lines, the poor proportions, and streaks in the paint. This place had been her sanctuary. Her pink haven was the place where she created the future she now wanted to live. But the designer clothes she imagined back then could only be purchased at sample sales, and the handsome man that was supposed to place her up on a pedestal hadn't materialized. Instead, she'd only managed to come across one dud after another. Why hadn't her mother told her there were more duds in the world than there were knights in shining armor?

The knock at the door disrupted her thoughts. "Dad?"

"Yeah, baby. Can I come in?" He peeked his head in.

"I thought you'd stay at the hospital."

"I only came home to change and to get your mother a gown so her backside won't be exposed." He held up a small bag.

She waved him in. He eased down on the edge of her bed. The drawn expression on his face made him look years older.

"Are you going to be okay?"

He pinched the bridge of his nose. "For our twenty-fifth anniversary, she wanted to go to an island. I should have taken her like she wanted. Now my knees are shot. I wouldn't be able to keep up with her even if I wanted to." He massaged his knees.

She reached out to grab his arm. "She's going to be fine. You'll get that chance. We just have to stay positive." She gave him a reassuring squeeze.

In an instance the grimace lines disappeared from his face, returning him to the rock-solid Dad that had all the answers. "I better get back to the hospital. I'll be there all day." He pointed to the stock pile of gifts her mother had placed in her room. "You'll get those wrapped for your mother, won't you?"

"Sure, Dad. Stop worrying."

"I hope you won't spend your whole day with your face in that computer. This is the holidays. Nobody is expecting you to work every day."

She lifted her eyebrows. "That's what you think," she muttered, but he was already out the door.

She shook her head and reached for her phone. She dialed her brother and listened to the rings.

"Where are you?" she said when Joshua picked up.

"Something's come up. I'll be there in a few days."

"A few days. Christmas Eve is a few days away and I need your help." She hated to beg. The weight was getting harder to bear. Everyone wanted something from her--Joshua, Keith, her father, and even her manager. When would someone be there to help her? Her college professor she'd met on the train was the only one extending assistance to her and, if history was any indication of the future, he probably wanted something too.

"I'll be there. Before Christmas," Joshua said. "Don't give me a hard time. Joanna and I are going through something right now. She's talking about leaving."

She took a deep breath. "I'm sorry, Joshua. What did you do this time?"

"Nothing. It wasn't me."

"You guys will work things out. You always do." Joshua could talk a homeless man out of his last penny. "You know Mom is in the hospital, don't you?" Panic was still in her voice. Since arriving at the hospital, everything that came out of her mouth was served with a side of tears. Joshua was still that little boy who thought the world circled around him and only came to life when he magically stepped forward with his presence. But with the pressure from her father, she had no patience for him to act like the little brother, today.

"Yes. I know, Bliss. I know they're running tests and her health may be worse than we knew. I don't see the need to rush up there if I can't do anything to help yet. I'll be there late tomorrow or sooner if something changes."

"But I need you, Joshua. Dad needs you. We should be here for him."

Her brother didn't respond. For a moment neither of them spoke.

"Bliss, calm down. I'm working on my own minor emergency here. I'll come up as soon as I can."

If another person told her to calm down she was certain she'd do just the opposite. She was wrapped so tight she was living in a straight-jacket. "Will you have my money?"

Another long silence extended between them. After several seconds he said, "I hope so. I'm working on it. Look, I've got to go. I'll call you later to see what's going on." His evasive mumbling was clear enough for her to know repayment was in jeopardy.

"Joshua, don't push me. I want my money and I want it just like you promised. Before Christmas." The unexpected edge in her voice surprised her, but the world was crowding her out.

"Yeah, I'll see what I can do." He ended the call.

Bliss stared at the cell phone. "I don't believe him." If her parents hadn't coddled him from the moment he was born, maybe he'd be a more responsible man. If he didn't fork over the money he owed her, then all her plans would fall through. All of them.

There were two texts from Keith, requesting she return his call. He'd been the one to end their fledgling relationship, why would she perform hurdles to call him? She shook her head and dropped the phone on the bed.

Her computer signaled the arrival of an email. She glanced down at the screen, clicked the envelope icon and quickly scanned the note. Her phone rang again.

Her manager's name was on the screen. With a resigned sigh, she accepted the call. "Roger, hello."

"Good morning Bliss. Can we meet at ten? In my office. I want to go over the Channel proposal. Our projections for next year are riding on it."

Her heart pounded so hard, talking was difficult. "Roger, I'm not in the city. I left yesterday to spend the holidays with my family." She talked as fast as her heart thumped. "I mentioned that to you."

There was an awkward silence. She could hear him breathing through the phone, making judgments on her because she wasn't sitting at her desk until Christmas morning, like Harry or that big brown noser, Daniel. He cleared his throat. Either the gesture was becoming an irritating habit or he was getting ready to lose his temper. "I agreed to give you the Channel account because I was assured you'd be in the office during this critical time."

"Roger, normally I don't take any extra time off at Christmas, but this year--"

"Bliss, I'm sure you think you have a good excuse. But the financial stability of the company is riding on this deal. I'm very hands on, I want to monitor your progress, and I can't do that if you're not here. Can you come back to the city today?"

She fast forwarded through the scenarios that would allow her to be back in the office until Christmas day. "Roger, I can't. My mother was rushed to the hospital yesterday. There is just no way." She swallowed. "But I promise the report will be on your desk before the New Year. I'll fax you what I have so far and you can call me to check in as often as you need. We can make this work."

For several moments he said nothing. "Don't screw this up." His voice was full of indignation. She could imagine the ugly expression on his face. "If you do--"

"I won't, Roger. I know how important this account is. I'll send you something today."

"Another thing." His tone was serious before, but now it had a heightened sense of foreboding. "You're aware of the investigation of Keith Richards."

She wanted to say no. The pit in her stomach told her to say no. But she couldn't lie to him. They had shown up together for the company picnic this summer. Another one of her not-so-bright ideas. She knew more about the investigation than she ever cared to reveal. "Yes. I am."

"Well, I got word this morning that the investigators want to talk to you after the holidays. Please tell me you didn't have anything to do with this mess. If word gets back to Chanel that the lead on their accounts was involved in some type of scandal, they will pull their business."

"I can assure you I don't know anything about doctoring documents. I've never even set foot in the labs. Why do they want to talk to me? I can't help them."

"They're talking to everyone that Keith knows."

"Well the two of us are no longer a couple. Of that, I can assure you." It was a good thing Roger couldn't see her face. She was certain he would have detected the lack of color from her brown face. She ended the call. She was being squeezed between two walls. Her home life and her personal life. Maybe by the time she was flattened, the churning in her stomach would stop.

She rubbed her eyes and left them closed for a moment to ease the stinging. Hours of reading small numbers on the spreadsheet and her eyes were as gritty as sand. If there was any magic in the holidays, she needed a dose right now.

Outside a car door closed. She scrambled off the bed to push aside the rose-colored curtain. A layer of snow had blanketed everything, giving the impression that the city had been turned into an enchanted snow village overnight. Marc stood beside his car, tightening the scarf around his neck against the falling snow-flakes. She studied him for a moment. Dr. Winbush driving her to the hospital. Dr. Winbush showing up at her house at ten in the morning as promised. None of her friends would believe her. Maybe she shouldn't believe this was happening either. For now, she'd just pretend this was normal.

She folded her arms under her breasts and gave him a more thorough exam. Yesterday had been such a blur she hadn't taken enough moments to notice him. Now she could examine him without his knowing. He was several years older than her. He didn't look old, he looked solid. Like a man who no longer questioned life but one who knew how to handle the ups and downs of it. The graying at his temples distinguished him from the average middle-aged man. The ones that walked around the office with privilege coursing through their veins. Marc took care of himself. For as long as she could remember her father had a pudgy stomach, but Marc 's stomach was as flat as the surface of a table. Maybe a quick look under his shirt would reveal rippled flesh like she'd seen on the cover of fitness magazines. A six or eight pack.

He made his way to the door and a moment later she heard the bell.

She charged down the stairs and opened the door. The moment her eyes locked with his, a familiar sensation ran through her. She couldn't be attracted to this man. He'd been her college professor. Wasn't there something off limits about him? The infatuation she had on him in college had melted away years ago. Hadn't it? He wasn't her type. The list of reasons disqualifying her reaction to him grew. He had gray hair, he was in his forties, and the ultimate deal breaker--he was married. But the way his gaze lingered on her breasts let her know he didn't care about any of those things. His presence unnerved her, he wasn't just looking at her, he was looking inside of her.

"Are you ready?" His smooth, creamy voice sounded different from the take charge person of yesterday.

"I just need to reply to one email then I'll be ready. Are the roads bad?"

"An email? Aren't you supposed to be on vacation?"

"It's my manager, questioning when the year-end report will be ready. Questioning everything I'm doing. I need to keep him assured that I can handle this account. As soon as I reply, I'll be ready."

"If we want to get through that list today, we need to hurry. Pretty soon shops will start to close because of the weather."

"It'll just take a minute. I've gotten a head start on the list. I placed an order with the market and they've promised to deliver the food this morning." She shot back up the stairs, even though there was disapproval on Marc's face. Answering to one man at a time was all she wanted to handle.

Getting the report out as promised was going to take divine intervention, but no way was she going to let Roger know that. Instead, she pounded out the answers he wanted to hear and sent the information she had, before coming back downstairs.

"Any word from your father?"

"He called this morning after he got back to the hospital. Her blood pressure is still too low, but the fluids have helped. No change, otherwise. She's still in a lot of pain. After we get the tree, I'd like to stop by and see her. I've made arrangements for a rental car while I'm here, so after we pick up the tree you can have your life back."

He nodded.

Bliss pulled on her coat and scarf before grabbing her purse. Together she and Marc made their way to his car. The wind bit at her exposed flesh.

"Do you think I'm crazy for trying to find a tree in this kind of weather?"

He placed his hand on her shoulder and gave her a reassuring pat. At the car, he held the passenger side door open for her before moving to the driver's side.

He pulled away from the curb, his eyes focused on the road. Men had a reason for everything they did. She needed to find out what Marc's reason was for inserting himself into the middle of her family drama. If it weren't for Christmas and her mother's demand that she come home this year, she wouldn't have come home this early. Arriving on Christmas Eve and leaving two days later would have given her more time to get her work done. "I still don't understand why you are doing this?"

"What?"

"Why would you take several hours out of your day to help me make my mother's wishes come true? You must have something better to do today." She stared at his face to see the things his words wouldn't reveal. "Don't you have friends you'd rather be with today?"

"I have several friends. But none of them need my help right now. Of all the people I know, you're the one who can benefit from my actions today. Why do you keep questioning me?" He glanced her way for a moment then turned his attention back to the road. "Aren't you enjoying my company?"

Those five words were loaded with meaning. She was enjoying everything about him. "I'm not used to people being so helpful. Usually, I have to beg people to do things for me. Everyone has an angle. I'm just trying to figure out what's in this for you."

"Maybe you need a new group of friends."

"Or a new brother. My father thinks he's going to come and help out. But I'll be lucky if I see Joshua on Christmas evening. He's not the kind of person that extends himself unless he's done a full personal risk, and benefit analysis."

"He's younger than you?"

"Yes, how did you guess?"

"Believe it or not, I used to be young and self-centered. Give him time, he'll get better."

Marc had a firm hold on life. He spoke with the confidence of a man that had figured out the ways of the world. Marc was probably self-assured when he was a thirteen-year-old boy.

They rode toward the city in quiet.

"You know all about me, why don't you tell me something about yourself? You mentioned your wife was from Delaware. But the way you let me flirt with you yesterday tells me, she's no longer in the picture or you're not the upstanding man you used to be."

"Why are you asking so many questions?"

"Because you're hanging out with me days before Christmas. If you had a wife, I imagine she'd have a list of things you'd need to do. Besides, I'm sure she wouldn't want you chauffeuring me around this morning."

"I was married. I'm not anymore." His tone was flat.

"Divorced?"

He knew enough about her. The need to level the playing field pushed her to keep asking questions.

He placed his right hand on top of the steering wheel and glanced at her. "My wife died five years ago." There was pain in his eyes.

Bliss swallowed. She'd done it again, pushed the boundaries a little too far. "I'm sorry, I shouldn't have asked." She paused. "It's just that you know all about my family and our dysfunction, I wanted to hear yours."

"What makes you think I have any dysfunction?"

"Every family has some. If you think you've missed that massive missile while cruising through life, just give me to end of the day and I'm sure I can pinpoint them for you."

He nodded, but his face tightened as if he was already trying to find a way to keep his secrets. "The Christmas tree lot is down here on the left. It's run by a Boy Scout Troop, so I figure by purchasing a tree here you're helping a good cause, too."

He found a parking space on the unpaved lot and turned off the car. "Are you ready? This should be fun, so stop looking like you're getting ready to face a firing squad."

"I've never shopped for a tree. This is something my mother and father did. I'm not ready to start taking over the things that were their responsibility. I always imagined this was something I'd do years from now, when they were much older."

He patted her knee, but his touch was so light there was nothing to be read into the gesture.

The sound of her cell phone filled the car. She opened her purse and pulled the noisy gadget free.

"Don't answer that," he said.

"Why not?"

"We're getting ready to do some Christmas tree shopping."

"Suppose it's my father...about, my mother?"

"Is it?"

She glanced at the screen. "It's Keith."

"Do you want to talk to him?"

"Should I? Is now a good time to give him that list of curse words I've been working on?"

His eyes turned toward the roof of the car like he was mulling over the question. "No. Let him wait a little longer. Men like for things to be difficult for them. Challenging. Are you okay with that?"

"Sure." She pushed the ringing phone back in her purse. "I've got enough going on right now. Talking to him only adds to my anxiety."

####

Marc followed Bliss as she walked from row to row showing no interest in any of the trees. With her gloved hands shoved deep in the pockets of her coat, she could have been window shopping on Fifth Avenue.

"Do you have any idea what kind of tree you want? Pine, Spruce, Fir?"

She faced him. "I have no idea. All I know is that it should be shaped like a triangle and it needs to be full." She examined a Pine tree that was already losing needles, then turned back to him. "Oh yeah, and it needs to smell good. I remember my mother always saying she wanted the house to have that evergreen smell."

"You don't want that one." He grabbed the tree she'd been examining and thumped it on the dirt lot. "This one is already starting to dry out. See all those needles." He pointed to the ground.

She threw her hands in the air. "You can see I know nothing about picking a tree." Her bottom lip dropped.

"Take a breath. You're just trying too hard. This is supposed to be fun." He grabbed her hand to lead her further down the path. "I think the most popular tree is a Fir and they smell wonderful." He selected two, holding one in each hand. "Which do you like the best?"

Her cell phone chimed. Without answering him, she pulled the phone from her purse. After a quick glance, she held up one finger before turning her back and addressing the caller.

He couldn't hear her conversation, but he was certain it wasn't her father or the hospital. He smacked his foot against the hard ground while waiting for her to end her call.

When she was done, she faced him. "Sorry about that. But I had to take that."

He nodded. "You remind me of my wife. Every time your phone rings you don't have to answer."

"I have to check. I could get an important call. At the firm, people who respond to email and calls while on vacation go further."

"And how do you know this?"

"Have you ever worked in corporate America?" The dubious expression on her face indicated she might have reached the limit of her patience.

"As a matter of fact, I did. For several years, after I left the University. And what I know is that people who don't manage their downtime eventually get taken down."

"Woooo, doesn't that sound fatal. I think I'm too young to worry about that right now."

"I wasn't born when George Washington was President you know. Forty is not as old as you think. I've been gray since my early twenties." He pushed his face past the tree limbs and closer to her. "See, no wrinkles."

She gave him a head to toe examination. She lingered at the crucial spots, his face, his hands and his crotch. And for the first time in a long time, he cared what someone else thought. What they saw. He wanted to be wanted.

"Are you done ogling me? You aren't being very discreet."

She stepped towards him. "I had to take a more meaningful look at you, now that I have more information about you."

"Did I pass?"

Her lips moved into a smile. "Yes. Now it's your turn. Tell me how old you think I am."

"Nope. I'm not playing that game."

"Why not?"

"I'm no fool. I'm sure if I guess wrong you won't be as gracious as I was."

"I'm twenty-seven."

"I was going to guess twenty-three."

"Liar."

He shook his head. This was a road he'd traveled before. Going down it again could be one helluva ride or one very bad idea. "Which tree?" he asked again over his thundering heart.

"Marc is that you?"

He knew the voice before he turned around.

"Yes, I thought that was you." His neighbor Lucy and her husband Floyd approached them.

Lucy threw her arms around Marc as if she hadn't seen him a few nights ago when she invited him over for a glass of Merlot when she knew he preferred Vodka.

"Lucy, Floyd. I want you to meet Bliss. I'm helping her pick out a Christmas tree." He tried to sound casual. With just a bit of information, Lucy would be off and running like a wildfire. Certain he was getting ready to get married.

Bliss stuck out her hand. The way Lucy evaluated her was only obvious to him. But Lucy was sizing her up, to see if Bliss measured up to her idea of a perfect replacement for Rachel.

"Aren't you a pretty thing?" Lucy said.

Bliss looked to him when she replied to Lucy. Her thank you was said so low Lucy might not have heard her, but Lucy was standing so close to Bliss she didn't miss a thing.

"How did you get this hermit to look for Christmas trees?" Lucy asked.

"I…I—"

"I offered, Lucy. I'm helping her out. Now stop being so nosy."

"Marc must bring you by our house during the holidays. On Christmas day we have this huge dinner. I'd love for you to come."

Floyd tugged on his wife's sleeve. "Honey, we'd better get going. I need to get home to let Bugsy out." Floyd directed his attention to Marc. "We've been tree hunting all morning. I'll bet the dog is ready to bust. Let's get a tree and get out of here, I think my toes are numb."

"Okay, Floyd. But I hope to see you and Marc at the house. Say you'll at least think about it," Lucy said.

"We'll think about, it," Marc replied.

Floyd pulled Lucy down another row of trees and out of sight.

"Why do I get the impression I was being evaluated?" Bliss stared at him.

"Because you were."

Chapter Four

Bliss helped Marc push the snow off the roof of the car. He hefted the large tree on top of the car like it was no heavier than a five-pound bag of potatoes. Together they tied the tree by looping the twine through the back windows of his small car. Her mother would be impressed with the hawking evergreen.

She and Marc hadn't spent many hours together and already something was different between them. Maybe it was his easy smile, or his optimistic approach to life, or that he'd stepped in to be her hero when no one else had.

He'd surpassed Keith by a thousand points. Marc was way better than any of her boyfriends, except Peter, who she'd loved in kindergarten. Peter had always shared his mother's chocolate chip cookies with her, which really wasn't a good barometer to measure anyone by, because none of them were ever in the running to meet her parents. They were just men to fill the few minutes she had between preparing quarterly reports and trying to break through the glass ceiling and recess.

After knotting the twine, he turned to her. "You're checking out my ass, aren't you?"

Her faced warmed. "I was. For a man your age, you're pretty nice."

He pushed his face within an inch of hers. "You're filling out those jeans pretty good yourself." He brushed his lips against hers. The gesture was so quick it could have been a friendly kiss, the kind she gave Aunt Clo. But the way her body warmed in the frigid temperature told her that was no ordinary kiss and they weren't just hanging out like pals.

"Now, if we don't hustle, we're not going to get through your list." He walked around her and opened the passenger side door until she climbed in. Without waiting for her to agree, he closed the door and disappeared to the driver side.

"Look, the snow is coming down heavier. We might have a white Christmas." Marc snapped his seatbelt and started the engine.

She took a deep breath. "That's all I need. Something else to complicate an already complicated situation."

With his hand resting on the steering wheel he said, "Bliss, a white Christmas is a good thing. Didn't all your childhood books show snow with Christmas?"

"Yeah, but I'm not a little girl anymore. My world can't stop because of snow, or even the holidays. Do you know I worked through the

Thanksgiving holiday? The closest I came to celebrating was the turkey sandwich from the vending machine at the office."

He drew back as if she'd tried to stab him. "Well, I can't let that happen for Christmas, now can I?"

She pulled the list from her purse. "If you hadn't decided to help me today, what would you be doing?"

"Writing."

"What?"

"I'm a writer. I'm finishing a story that is due to my publisher the first of the year."

"Oh, so I'm not the only one with deadlines. You should be more sympathetic to what I'm going through."

His face relaxed and the beginning of a smile took over. Being around him elevated her mood.

"I've got very clear boundaries. My life isn't ruled by my phone or by what someone else wants me to do." He looked at her just long enough for her to see his sincerity.

"Are you independently wealthy?"

He titled his head. "Let's say I'm alright."

"Well, if I was alright, I wouldn't care either. I'm one of those people who is almost living from paycheck to paycheck. Stop for a minute and imagine how scary that is living in Manhattan. Maybe you're being too critical of a situation you don't fully understand."

"You might have a point. But I also have a really good idea how precious life is and how it can change in a second. I'm not one to waste time."

The snow had picked up. Instead of the fine flakes, now they were heavy and thick. Marc sped up the windshield wipers, but it was hard to see against the blanket of white.

They were quiet for several minutes. Marc's attention was focused on the road that was now coated in a mixture of snow and road dirt.

His words weren't harsh, but he had no idea what she was going through. Having just enough money to cover the bills and hoping no emergencies popped up that would throw her whole life into a downward spiral kept her stomach in one large knot. If Joshua didn't come through with the money he owed her, catching a train back to New York could be the genesis of a whole set of new problems.

"I guess we should do some gift shopping next," she said without looking up.

"We should get the tree in water as soon as possible. It was probably cut down over a month ago and shipped here. After we get it in the stand we can tackle the next thing on your list. The weather is turning bad so we should get as much done today as we can."

She dropped the list to reach for her ringing phone.

"Are you going to answer that?"

"Without replying, she slid her finger across the screen to take the call. Her manager's voice boomed through the phone. "Bliss, I want to go over the numbers again with you. I'm looking at last month's report and something is not adding up."

Her stomach tightened around each of his words. If she were in New York, juggling all the demands would have been part of the normal routine. But from the moment the train deposited her on the platform nothing had been normal. Nothing. Her nose stung, but no matter what, she refused to cry.

Marc pulled to a stop in front of the house and turned off the car.

"Eric, hold on a second." She placed her hand over the mouth-piece and fished the house keys from the side pocket of her purse. "Go on in, I'll be right there. I set the tree stand in front of the living room window."

"You want me to start without you?" There was a cross tone in his voice.

"I know I'm asking for too much. But I...I..." she croaked.

"I got this. Take your call. I'll wait for you inside."

####

Marc glanced over his shoulder before unlocking the front door. She was another generation, with different values. People her age bounced from one relationship to the next. Everything about her screamed heartbreak. She'd return to New York after Christmas and think the fling she had with her college professor was a hoot.

He kicked the snow off his boots then pushed the huge tree into the living room. He returned to the porch to carry in the groceries she'd ordered. She was so absorbed in her conversation she didn't even look his way.

The groceries she'd order earlier were stacked next to the door. With the temperature in the teens, there was no worry about anything spoiling.

The stress she was going through was obvious, she looked like she thought the world was going to gobble her up if she stopped long enough to take a breath. He had plenty of reasons to say bye and head to his quiet home, but none of them were as vibrant and alluring as Bliss. The last time a woman cinched him like this, he ended up marrying her. And even though the end was a walk through hell, he'd do it all over again, and something about Bliss promised him the happiness he deserved.

Bliss's life was as screwed up as his used to be. Her priorities were focused on things that would evaporate and leave her with nothing but a handful of emptiness. Maybe he could find a way to save her from herself.

He couldn't shake her from his thoughts. Without even trying, she'd anchored something in him. Maybe it was the need to save her from what he'd been through, or maybe it was because of the undeniable feelings that started brewing for her the moment she talked to him on the train. She was as infectious as a smiling baby.

He unloaded the boxes on the kitchen counter and returned to the living room. From the window, he watched her still seated in the car. Her hands and mouth moved with more animation than she'd used to select the Christmas tree. Whatever point she was trying to make, there was no lack of passion in her argument.

Snow whipped around the car. A blanket already covered the hood and the windshield. Nothing else was going to get done today. The idea of being snowed in with Bliss was both exhilarating and frightening. How could he trust his emotions when they had been dormant for so long? The last thing Bliss needed was another jerk in her life, and maybe all he needed was a good lay.

He shook his head before walking away. His best option was to stay quiet and move on as soon as a chance presented itself. As soon as she pulled out her computer to start toiling away on something she thought was more important. As soon as she loosened her grip on him to allow him to think like the wise man he thought himself to be. But he knew he wouldn't. As if a white super-hero cape was draped around his shoulder, he needed to show her how to relax, how to enjoy life, how to set herself free. He wanted her in his bed under him, on top of him.

By the time Bliss came through the front door of the house, the tree was secure in the stand and he'd added the water to the base.

"I'm so sorry, Marc," she gushed, and removed her coat and scarf. "I didn't think the conversation would last that long." There was genuine regret in her eyes. The grocery list dangled from her right hand.

"Not a problem." He didn't want to sound curt, but he couldn't resist it either. "Look, I'd better get going." He made a move toward the door, even though he knew he wouldn't abandon her. He only wished he could.

Her face flushed. She folded her bottom lip under her teeth and stared at the tree. She wasn't crying, but with just a little provocation the tears would start to flow. This was the perfect time to escape, to get back to his simple existence where the only person that required answers was himself. She was too young, too naive. He made a move toward the door and halted before opening it.

"Did something happen?" he asked without turning to face her or taking his hand off the knob.

There was still an opportunity for him to get to the tranquility of his everyday life. But he couldn't leave her. Not with his desire for her mounting by the minute.

"What am I doing? Why am I doing this? I can't make the Christmas magic like my mother. I'm not even sure I believe in Christmas magic." Her voice was barely audible, but it pulled him back into the room.

He crossed the room to stand near the chair where she had flopped. He placed his hands on her shoulders. She stared at the floor and made a sound that was half wail and half moan. He knelt beside the chair and took her hand in his. Her fingers were cold. Why was he always attracted to the ones that needed fixing? Why hadn't staying at Rachel's side, watching as she let her life fall apart a piece at a time been enough?

The only items crossed off the list were the Christmas tree and the grocery shopping. He removed the piece of paper from her hand. Even though there were only three major things left to be done, it might as well have been one hundred. She was in no more shape to tackle the tasks, then he was of abandoning her to do them alone. She pulled off her snow-caked boots and left them by the door.

He pulled her against his chest. With his free hand, he stroked her face. Her skin was as soft as he'd imagined. "Bliss." He held her tighter. With a slight turn of her head, she pulled him in with a blank expression. He knew the kind of emotion she was wrestling with. That moment when you want to be numb, so that bad news or unhappiness won't penetrate that little place in your heart that's full of hope.

She glanced at him but remained tucked against him. Her eyes were unfocused. He wasn't even sure she'd heard him until she pressed her lips to his. He couldn't pull away from soft, moist lips. He slipped his tongue in her mouth and everything around them went quiet. There was only the two of them in the whole world. In that instant, they fused together like two people looking for refuge in a storm.

Her hands cupped his face, deepening the kiss. She'd caught him off guard. One moment she was on the brink of tears, now she was ravaging his tongue as if it were her life-line to happiness. He moved his hands under her sweater. Her skimpy bra did little to cover the soft mounds of flesh. Without releasing his mouth, she moaned softly, it was both lustful and wanting.

He helped her out of her coat and pulled her sweater over her head. He tried to remember the last time the need to be with someone had consumed him in such a tremendous way. Months before Rachel started showing signs of sickness.

Bliss reached for his belt bucket. She struggled to loosen the clasp.

"Let me help you with that," he said.

"Let's go upstairs, to my bedroom." Her voice was husky.

"Are you sure you want to do this?" A moment ago, she was flustered. Taking advantage of her now would be despicable. "Besides, I don't have any protection."

"Between my bedroom and my brother's childhood bedroom, I'm sure I'll find something." She grabbed his hand. "I've wanted to do this since last night." She led him up the stairs.

At the top of the landing, she left him and crossed the hall. He could hear the opening and closing of drawers.

"I knew I'd find something. Let's hope these condoms haven't dry rotted." She held up three foiled packs.

In what could only be her room, she closed the door. After removing her bra she kicked off her shoes then removed her jeans. In the vanishing light of the setting sun, her skin glowed like brand new copper pennies.

"You're staring." She looked down at her toes. They were painted the same vibrant red as her fingernails.

"I can't help it. You look just as good with your clothes off as you do with them on."

"Take off your clothes and let me see if I can say the same thing about you."

She pulled his t-shirt over his head. This time she had no problems with his belt. When he stepped out of his remaining clothes, she ran her hand along his stomach. "You look exactly the way I thought you would. I'll bet I can find a naked picture of you buried somewhere in one of my college notebooks."

"Why bother when you've got me right here." He backed her up to the bed and came down on top of her. Bliss didn't see him as the sad man carrying around the spirit of his dead wife. To her, he was still that strapping young buck that used to teach marketing to half-interested twenty-somethings. He wanted to live up to every one of her expectations, but his lust mounted with each breath. If he didn't slow down they'd both be disappointed.

He stopped at her neck, kissing every inch of the long column. The scent of Jasmine and vanilla emanated from her flesh. She planted kisses across his chest, her legs tightened around his back. Five years was a lot of time to make up. There had been women, plenty of women, but they were all for functional purposes. Just to provide a release for his pent-up libido. Bliss was pure pleasure. Pleasure that he'd denied for too many years.

She loosened her legs, giving him the ability to explore more of her body. He kissed the flat plane of her stomach then continued between her legs. She lifted her hips, giving him easier access to the part of her he wanted to taste. He inserted his tongue into her moist opening. Every touch breathed life back into his soul. Her moans filled the room. The sound encouraged him to delve deeper. He wanted to please her. Being able to focus his attention on someone else was the medicine he needed. Her body quivered with each thrust of his tongue.

With his internal wounds so deep, and the thirteen-year age gap, maybe he was fantasizing that someone as youthful as Bliss would be halfway interested in him. But he'd examine his motivation another time. When his head was clear and his body wasn't exploding with need.

She bucked her hips like a filly being freed from a pen. Her body shook with such velocity, a degree of satisfaction raced through him that matched her. Then she lay still on the mattress. Her chest rose and fell as if she'd just finished a marathon. For several minutes, the sound of their breathing filled the room. There was joy in their quiet moment together.

He climbed beside her to catch his breath too. "I wasn't expecting that."

"Neither was I. But I'm not going to complain." She rubbed her hand over his chest and stomach. With no preamble, she climbed on top of him. "I'm not a selfish lover."

"I don't think there is anything selfish about you."

"Let me show how giving I can be." The kisses she planted on his chest were warm. She gripped a fist full of his hair and pulled him up. With a firm grip on his penis, she massaged his shaft. The hope he had of stretching the moment to eternity was fading.

He slid the condom into place then rolled her over and buried his penis deep inside her. The heat that surrounded him was intoxicating. He wanted to linger in the moment, but she moved her hips. Together they swayed, giving and taking in what seemed like equal amounts. She couldn't be holding back because he couldn't handle any more. Each thrust was a step closer to ecstasy. The way her fingers dug into his back said she was feeling the same way.

Warmth washed over him, covering his body in a slow wave of pleasure so intense every muscle in his body tightened. By the time it reached his loins, he was transported to a place where there was no easy retreat.

There was no hurry to get dressed or go back downstairs. Her bedroom had become a sanctuary, and leaving the peacefulness to step back into reality was nothing to rush into. Here they could pretend to be anything they wanted and he was good at masquerading. Wasn't he duping her right now into thinking he was normal? Not a man carrying around the soul of his dead wife, unable to let her go and live the life she wanted for him? If ever he was going to release Rachel and move on with his life, this was the time. But thinking there was a future with Bliss was too crazy, even for him.

"Now what?" She reached into her closet and pulled a blue sweater from the hanger.

"We can do whatever you want. For the balance of the day, let's say I'm all yours."

The expression on her face melted into a picture of thankfulness. Looking at her now, it was easy to understand how she had enchanted him.

Back in the living room, she rushed to pull her ringing phone from her purse. Too bad the mellow atmosphere they'd shared upstairs wasn't transferred down here.

"I don't think I've ever met anyone whose phone commands their life as much as yours."

"That's because you're old and you think cell phones are only for emergency, like when you have a flat tire on the side of the road."

"No. It's because I won't let a little palm-sized gadget rule my life."

"At least no one called while we were busy." She put the nuisance to her ear. After a series of nods, she ended the call. "That was my Dad. He said my mother is doing better. She may be home tomorrow." Joy lit up her face. The glow she wore a minute ago intensified.

"That's great news."

"But I have so much to do. I need to trim the tree, wrap the gifts, and start preparing for dinner.

Tomorrow is Christmas Eve and there is so much to be done."

The need to be her hero surged in his chest. He gathered her in his arms. "I'll tell you what. Let's go to the hospital now so you can see your mother before the weather gets much worse. Then we can spend the rest of the night trimming the tree and whatever else needs to get done." He heard the words as he spoke them and they sounded foreign to his ears. He was digging in deeper. "How does that plan sound?"

"Dad said to give them an hour or so. She's not in the room right now."

"That's fine." He released her. "Stay right there. I'm going to get you some water. He made his way to the kitchen, found the cabinet that contained a shelf of small plastic glasses, the kind you use if you have a house full of children. He filled it with water from the refrigerator before making his way back to her. She was seated in the chair, staring down at the puddle left by the snow that had melted off her boots onto the floor. He pressed the hard plastic cup into her hand and forced her to take a sip.

"Maybe my mother is right. Maybe there is something magical about Christmas. For the first time since I've stepped off the train, I feel like anything is possible." She lifted her head to stare at him. "I want to take you back upstairs, crawl under the cover and stay there. But--"

"We've been dancing around each other all day. If you hadn't kissed me, I was going to kiss you."

She slipped her hand under his shirt. "Maybe you're my Christmas magic." Her voice wobbled even though her eyes blazed with renewed light.

There were no ropes around his ankles. He was being pulled under and every moment with her was exactly what he wanted. Offering Bliss a ride was the first moment his life had picked up momentum. If there was a mirror in front of him, he wouldn't recognize the stranger staring back at him.

The doorbell disrupted the quiet in the house. Without saying anything he made his way to the door and opened it.

"May I help you?"

"Hi, I'm here to talk to Bliss Duncan. Do I have the right place?"

Chapter Five

At the sound of his voice, a wave of dampness washed over her neck and shoulders. Bliss froze. She couldn't go to the door or retreat to the kitchen. She didn't know what kind of person she should be with him. Should she be angry with him? There was no remorse about the break-up. But why couldn't he have stayed in New York? Delaware was off limits to him. Since he didn't come when she invited him, he had no right to come when she was already moving on. It was as if he had some kind of radar and could tell she was getting ready to cross over into a place where he wasn't welcome. Did he sense that she was falling for someone else? Someone unlike him? Someone who was willing to put her first.

Why was he here? What did he want? She closed her eyes for a brief moment, gathering her wits before making her way to the door.

"Keith, why are you here?"

He started across the room with his arms stretched out as if hugging her was always his first reaction. She held up her hands.

"Whoa, Keith. What are you doing here?" she asked again and stepped back.

"Because you wouldn't return my calls or answer my text." His eyes narrowed. Marc stood between the two of them. She wanted to reach for Marc's hand, needing some of the steadiness that seemed to radiate from him.

"Keith, nice to meet you." Marc stuck out his hand. "I'm Marc Winbush."

Keith hesitated before shaking his hand, looking first at her and then back to Marc. If she was supposed to be happy to see Keith, those emotions were buried and didn't materialize. He was even more haggard now than when she'd left New York. The bags under his eyes were more noticeable. His skin was a disturbing shade of gray. His slacks and shirt were neat and fresh, but for him, that was always easy. Keith prided himself on his wardrobe. But if he came here to burden her with more of his work melodrama, he wouldn't be happy with what she had in store for him.

Their constant bickering over menial things had been lost in the easy camaraderie she found with Marc. The two men standing at the front door of her parent's house were as different as the seasons. Marc was taller. Keith was younger. Marc's hair was salt and pepper. Keith's head was almost clean shaven. Marc was unraveled by the appearance of Keith. Keith was rattled that she hadn't welcomed him by throwing her arms around his neck and thanking him for coming to her rescue. She sucked her tongue at the thought.

"This really isn't a good time. You shouldn't have come."

"Bliss, would you like for me to leave you two alone?" Marc released the door handle.

"No." Bliss placed her hand on his arm. "How did you get here?"

"I caught a cab from the train station."

"What do you want? You broke up with me. There isn't anything else that needs to be said."

Keith pushed his hands into his coat pocket. "I was trying to get your attention. I thought if I did something dramatic, you'd stop long enough to talk to me. Are you going to let me in? In case you hadn't notice, there is a blizzard out here." He pointed over his shoulder. His footsteps leading to the door were disappearing in the falling snow.

"We were just getting ready to leave," Marc said.

Keith drew back and examined her and Marc. His eyes raked over him with closer attention this time. She could almost read the thoughts as his brain processed the situation.

"Excuse me," Keith started. "Bliss, what is going on here?"

"I'm a friend of Bliss'" Marc spoke up.

"What kind of friend?" Keith turned his attention to Bliss.

"Keith, like I said, this is not a good time. I'm on my way to the hospital to see my mother. You shouldn't have just shown up here. And the minute you broke up with me, you lost the right to ask me questions."

"Well, I don't think you're going anywhere right now." Keith looked back over his shoulder. "There's a state of emergency and everyone should stay off the roads."

Keith stepped over the threshold and Marc closed the door.

"I'm sorry about your mother. I hope it's nothing too serious." Keith reached for her hand. His cold fingers enclosed hers, stealing her warmth.

"Bliss, this is your call. What do you want to do? If seeing your mother is important, then I'll get you to the hospital." Marc tightened the front of his coat.

Keith snapped straighter. "I can take you." He turned to Marc. "You can push off now, Marc. Whatever she needs, I can take care of it for her."

The door opened and her brother Joshua trudged in. "Hey, what's going on here? I just left Mom and she was fine. Did something just happen?" He pulled the cap off his head and shook the snow off.

"No. This has nothing to do with Mom."

"Then why are you all standing by the door. And who are these people?" Joshua stepped further into the room and nodded his head at the two men.

"Marc has been helping me since I came home—Marc Winbush."

Marc embraced Joshua in a hardy handshake. "I've heard a lot about you. Glad to finally meet you, Joshua."

She pointed to Keith. "And this is my ex-boyfriend. I'm still trying to figure out what he's doing here?"

Marc draped his arm over her shoulder and gave her a firm squeeze. The gesture boosted her sagging disposition. There was something troubling about Keith being at the house. The way he kept fidgeting and the way his eyes darted around the room, one would have thought he was expecting the sky to fall on him.

Joshua grabbed her by the hand and pulled her into the kitchen.

"Are you sure everything is okay here?" He glanced over his shoulder toward the door. "All that looks a little strange."

She unbuttoned her coat and used her hands to fan her face. "Since I've gotten home everything is weird."

"I'll say." Joshua pulled off his coat and placed it on the back of the chair before sitting. "So how long have you been dating the weird one?"

"Keith's not weird. He's just going through something at work and he is expecting me to hold his hand through it. But since I decided to come home, he's bugging out."

"He's bugging out because he's high. I didn't know you were into that kind of guy. Is that why you're pressing me for the money? You're not--"

"Of course not." She flopped in the chair next to him. "Get outta here." She swatted his arm. "Keith doesn't do drugs. Why would you say that? How would you know?" Her words came out in a whoosh of wind.

Joshua shrugged his shoulders. "Don't flip out on me, sis and keep your voice down. I'm just telling you what I think. If he's not on drugs, something has got him wired."

"It's his job. He's been stressed out about it for months." She pushed her hair off her forehead and rubbed her eyes. "Why he decided to drag that here for the holidays is crazy. I've got my own drama. Maybe I can talk him into going back to New York."

"Nobody is going anywhere anytime soon. So, you better find a way to deal with having both of your men here. And since we're all going to be stuck here for a while, I'd advise you to handle it with care." Joshua pulled off his sweater.

She dropped her head into her hands. "Ugh. I don't think I can handle all of this right now. Why are men so needy?"

"Because women like to nurture us. We're just giving you what you want." He smirked.

She cut her eyes at her brother. "That's some bull. Women end up being the caretakers because if we didn't, nobody would." She slumped against the chair, exhaustion consuming her. "Tell me what happened at the hospital."

"Mom is doing fine. The test results all came back negative, so there isn't anything major wrong with her. Other than the leg and ankle. She might even be home for Christmas."

The weight sitting on her shoulders since she stepped off the train station loosened its grip on her. She exhaled from her mouth, taking her time and allowing her body to absorb the good news. She flopped in the chair on top of his coat. "That is the best thing I've heard in days. If she's home, then maybe I can call off this charade of the Merry Christmas."

"What about the two boyfriends in the living room? What are you going to do about them?"

She drew her head back. "Keith broke up with me by text message a few days ago, so he is no longer my boyfriend."

"Ouch!"

"And Marc used to be my professor. We were on the same train, so we're reconnecting. He's just a friend, helping with my long to-do list since you were unavailable." She didn't mask the sarcasm in her voice.

Joshua reached in the refrigerator and pulled out a carton of milk. He took a long pull from the carton. "You might think you're friends, but that man has other ideas."

He placed the milk back in the refrigerator.

"That is gross, Joshua. Nobody wants to drink after you." She jumped up, removed the carton from the refrigerator and poured the contents down the drain. "Now I see why you're still single. Grow up, dude."

He smirked. "I see you're still bossy as hell. Just so you know, Mom keeps milk in the refrigerator just for me." He turned the carton around and pointed to the big "J" scribbled on the side.

"I should have known. That's why you've never grown up, because our parents keep babying you." She returned to the chair. "And why do you think Marc likes me."

He sat across from her. "Men know these things. You shouldn't leave the two of them in there too long. They might decide to duel for your honor." He chuckled.

####

Marc removed his coat and sat on the living room sofa. He shifted until he was comfortable. One thing he had in abundance was patience. And whatever was going on here today required an extra dose

He studied Keith, who continued to stand at the door as if he was waiting on instructions on what was supposed to happen next. He was the kind of man Bliss would go for, tall, good-looking, but with no depth of character. He was as high strung as she was. From the moment he walked in, some part of him was in constant motion. Now he was rolling his thumbs against each other trying to overhear the conversation taking place in the kitchen.

With his foot crossed over his knee, he tried to dissect the situation. Nothing about Keith should have bothered him, but everything about him was abrasive. Maybe it was his youth. Keith was so certain that he would always be young and life wouldn't serve him a dirty hand that he stunk with entitlement. The smugness of his appearance here. Did he think just because he made the effort to show up that Bliss had to forgive him for his callous behavior? Marc shook his head. Too bad women didn't know more about chivalry and what their minimum expectation should be from the men in their lives. Bliss deserved much better than Keith could ever give her.

"You might as well take a seat. I think we're going to be here for a while." Marc called to him. "At least until the roads are cleared."

There was only one way to describe the look Keith gave him.

Annoyed.

Keith entered the living room and sat in the chair furthest from Marc. He sat straight up like he was being interviewed for a job. Could compete with Keith? Understanding her attraction to Keith may be difficult to comprehend, but there was something about him that Bliss must have liked.

"Did she tell you about me?" Keith started rolling his thumbs again.

"Not much. It was pretty gallant of you to drive all the way down here in a blizzard. You must really love her."

Keith's face tightened. For the first time since arriving, some body part wasn't in motion. "We...I..." He coughed in his hand. "We haven't been dating too long, but I care about her. I know it was pretty harsh the way I broke things off with her and I needed to apologize to her."

"Still, to drive two hours for an apology, two days before Christmas, in a snow-storm, that must mean something."

"Look buddy." Keith leaned forward.

"Marc. My name is Marc."

"Yeah, Marc. You got a thing for Bliss?"

Marc let the question loose in his head for a moment. He hadn't had a thing for anyone in so long he was sure he could identify the emotion. Rachel's death had left him numb and he'd grown so used to feeling nothing, it was like slipping on a pair of well-worn slippers. "I do. I have a thing for Bliss." He nodded his head, liking the way the sensation shot through him.

"And I guess she's diggin' on you?"

"I don't know. I haven't asked her."

"You old geezers don't waste much time, do you?"

Marc snorted without opening his mouth. "I've never wasted time."

Bliss walked in the living room with her brother right behind her.

Keith jumped up. "So now what?" He rubbed his hands together. "What are we going to do?"

Joshua gave Keith a solid pat on the back. "You might as well take off your coat. I think we're going to be here for a while. Maybe even overnight. But I hope you don't expect to be entertained. I don't think anyone is up for that."

"I can't stay here overnight. I need to get back to New York." Keith looked from Marc and over at Bliss. "I just want to spend a little time with you, Bliss."

"I still don't understand why you even came, Keith. I asked you to come with me to celebrate the holidays and you all but said you'd rather eat dirt. If you want to try to make it back to New York in this weather, go ahead." Bliss motioned to the door.

"Can I talk to you alone for a moment? " Keith asked.

"No, not right now." She took a step back out of the room. "My head is starting to pound. I need to find Mom's pain relievers. I'll search the medicine cabinet. Will you guys be okay?"

"Go ahead. I'll keep Marc and Keith company with my witty repartee." Joshua flopped on the sofa at the opposite end of Marc and waved his sister away.

Chapter Six

Bliss found the familiar brand of generic pain relievers her parents always bought. At the bathroom sink, she cupped her hand under the running water then she threw her head back to swallow the pills.

In her bedroom, she collapsed on the bed. How could time be moving fast and slow at the same time? With Marc, she wanted to move things along. Test him out like you test drive a new car. With Keith, she wanted to slow things down. Give herself the time she needed to see the kind of man he was, not the man she hoped he was. She smacked her knee. She should have broken things off with him long ago. Right after that incident with Megan.

The chill in the air penetrated her bones. The cold had settled under her skin and would be there until spring. There was something about winter that made it her least favorite season. Maybe it was the way the wind stole her words or the extra layers of clothes that weighed her down and made it impossible to feel anything. No matter what it was, she wasn't looking forward to the coming months.

She dug herself deeper into the down bedding trying to warm herself. Her mother thought Christmas was magical. In the quiet of her room, she tried to summon forth the optimism of her mother and her grandmother. The gifts that her mother had bought were piled against the bedroom wall. Sometime in the next few days, she'd need to start wrapping those gifts.

The soft murmurs of men whiffed up the stairs and into her room. Marc, Keith, and Joshua, strangers to each other and to her in many ways. What could they be talking about? Her? They had little else in common. Would Keith tell them how unsupportive she was? Would Joshua tell them how she kept hounding him to pay back the loan that he had no intention of repaying? Would Marc tell them how he was in the wrong place at the wrong time and had gotten swept up into the drama?

She flopped on her side and stared up through the window. The wind howled louder and the snow had turned into big, fat flakes that looked as if they had been hand cut. She closed her eyes. Sleep was impossible and so was the idea of relaxing. The notion of slowing down and unwinding was as foreign to her as everything else that had happened so far.

The only thing she'd done all day was visit her mother and pick out a tree. Her mother was doing better, but the tree wouldn't be up to Mom's standards.

With Christmas just two days away, hoping that everything would turn out like one her mother had planned was impossible. But she would try.

If she had to choose between hurt or angry, she'd have a hard time choosing. With Keith, she was angry. He had no business showing up. Was the man that needy? Things would have been so much simpler if he had stayed broken-up with her like he'd said in his text. Now she was forced to deal with him.

With Joshua, she was hurt. How could he borrow money he had no intention of paying back? And what was she supposed to do now about her rent and credit card bill?

For once, Mom and Dad weren't on the list. She squeezed her eyes together. For them she was afraid. Both of them needed to be well, and happy and healthy, the way they always were and the way she always wanted them to be. If there was any magic in the holidays, that's where it needed to be.

There was no use in wishing she could snap her fingers and stop the snow, and send Keith away and make Joshua pay up, and make her mother well, and Marc her hero. Grown-up and grown-up problems never vanished in a poof of mist. She was supposed to square her shoulders and address her issues like the fully developed woman she claimed to be.

She pushed the comforter away and sat up. Her little pink haven couldn't wrap her up like a cocoon and make her happy like it did when she was fifteen and Bobby Gibbs refused to come to her sweet sixteen party. Nothing was as easily fixed as the problems she had back then.

Footsteps sounded on the hardwood of the stairs. No doubt someone on a quest to disrupt her quiet moment.

"Bliss, where are you?" Keith was whispering and a picture of him on his tiptoes flashed in her head.

"I'm in here, Keith."

He peeked his head in the door before stepping inside. Even though he was dressed in his normal attire of slacks and a buttoned-down shirt there was something disheveled about him. Maybe it was his hawk appearance in her childhood bedroom, but he looked out of place, as if all his nerves were exposed. What had she ever been attracted to in him? Or was she so desperate not to be alone, she'd relaxed, or ignored, her standards just to have someone sit across the table from her?

"What do you want?" She had about as much enthusiasm for him as he'd had for her when he sent his infamous text.

He sat on the edge of the bed. "I came here to talk to you. I wanted to say I'm sorry."

She nodded.

"I'm going through some stuff."

"I know. You've told me that every day for the last two months." She placed her hands in her lap.

The sooner this conversation ended, the sooner she could be back to fulfilling the things on her mother's list. "Are you using drugs?"

"No." He drew away from her. "Why the hell would you ask me that?"

"Never mind. Are you done?"

He looked around the room. "Where is your purse?"

"Why? If you want to borrow money, you're too late. I don't have any."

"No. I don't want money. I...I...misplaced something and I thought it might be in your purse."

She examined his face, trying to see what Joshua thought he saw. His eyes didn't look buggy, nor was he scratching, but he was fidgety. "Why would something *you* lost be in *my* purse?"

She reached across the bed for her bag.

"Never mind. I've been looking everywhere." He shook his head. "Forget it. Can we just talk?"

She massaged the bridge of her nose. "Look. We know our relationship was stalled. We were both unhappy and you breaking up with me was a good thing. Maybe you could have found a better way to do it, just in case you ever need to do it again. But I think it was best for us."

He dropped his head and stared into his palms. "This thing at work...it could have been an accident...I mean..."

"What do you mean it could be an accident? You told me you checked the reports several times and you signed off."

He shot out of the chair and stared out the window. "I did." His voice faltered, cracking with the same lack of conviction that he used to explain the phone calls and meetings with Megan.

Her heart lay heavy in her chest, like a misplaced object. How was she always drawn to the damaged ones? The men that couldn't commit, that wanted someone to cater to them instead of just love them. The men that were never satisfied with just one woman, the men that didn't know the meaning of truth and honesty, that thought it was some obscure virtue that was only talked about but never practiced.

"You falsified those records, didn't you, Keith? You put all those trials in danger. And the company." She stood and moved away from him. With the bed between them, maybe she could see Keith with a clearer head and purer eyes.

He spun around. "No...I...no." His eyes narrowed. He was sorry he'd let his guard slip. But she knew him. He only stumbled over his words when he was making them up.

"How could you, Keith?" she yelled.

He lurched across the room and snatched her purse off the bed.

She tried to yank it from him. "What are you doing? Give me that."

He held it just beyond her reach. He fished inside, throwing out her wallet, her cosmetic bag, followed by her cell phone and charger.

"What are you looking for?" She streaked at him. This Keith she didn't know, she didn't recognize. The well-put-together man, who was supposed to have a handle on his life was now as strange as his behavior.

His eyes glazed over and he continued throwing the contents of her purse on the bed. He was so deep in his own head he probably didn't even hear her.

Marc and Joshua came through her bedroom door.

"What's going on here? I heard you yell." Marc stood beside her, putting his arm around her shoulder like it was natural as if they had long ago moved from being friends to being something more.

Keith flanked the other side of her.

"He's acting like a mad-man." She nodded towards Keith, who was now removing her pens and journals.

Marc approached him and yanked her purse away, but not before he removed a folded piece of paper. Keith seemed to shrink the moment he held the paper. The mania eased out of his body like he'd been pierced, deflating him like an old balloon.

"What's going on with you, man? Are you okay?" Marc asked.

Keith stared at them

Joshua slipped across the room and wrenched the paper from Keith's hand. "So, what is this all about?" Joshua unfolded the edges and studied the paper. The little lines in his forehead grew deeper.

Keith slumped on the bed, burying his head in his hands. If her heart weren't pounding over time, she might have been able to summon up some pity for him. But his berserk behavior had worn away any emotion she could have mustered for him.

"Sis, did you read this?" Joshua asked without looking up.

"What is it?"

"This was written to you, and I think you ought to read it." Joshua handed the note to her with a backward glance at Keith. Her younger brother may treat her like a jerk, but he never let anyone else mistreat her. From the hunch of his shoulders, he was ready to pounce on Keith, but Keith already looked defeated.

She skimmed the letter. Her heartbeat increased with each line. "Keith." His name escaped from her mouth without her even trying. She reread the letter. Absorbing the words this time.

"Is this your suicide note?" She brandished the paper in his direction. He didn't respond. "Answer me, Keith. So, you did falsify all those records. Putting helpless people in jeopardy. The company will prosecute, you'll go to jail." She looked down at the paper, again. "And Megan. You even admitted to screwing Megan, but you made me believe I was paranoid and insufficient."

"I couldn't do it," Keith mumbled without lifting his head. "By the time you read that letter, I was supposed to be gone. I had everything all planned. It was supposed to look like an accident."

She couldn't find any words for him. Her mouth opened but without anything constructive to say, she snapped it shut and turned to Marc. If her family drama hadn't been enough to send him fleeing, this new turn of events should do the trick.

Marc reached for Keith's elbow and helped him up. "Let's go downstairs where we can sit and talk."

"I'm not sure I want to be in the same room with him. He cheated. He lied. I don't even know who he is." Bliss pressed her back against the wall. "What if the company thinks I have something to do with all this? That I knew?"

"We'll sort it all out." Marc was calm. They could have been discussing the price of bread. "One thing is for sure, we're all stuck here for the time being."

Bliss led the way back to the first floor. Her mind tried to process what was going on. Bits of sentences and scenarios ran through her head like rapid gunfire. What had she missed? Why hadn't she been able to put the pieces together? Had she been so smitten by Keith's good looks that she didn't think he was capable of being a liar and a cheat? Was she so happy to grace his arm, she'd overlooked his shortcomings on purpose? When had she become one of those women that accepted anything and everything just to be able to have a date on Saturday night?

She wasn't certain if she was more disappointed in Keith or herself.

####

Bliss rushed to the single chair furthest from the sofa and flopped into it, tucking her feet under her. Just when she thought she could manage through her mother's crisis, another one landed at her feet. This Christmas was anything but magical. So far it was turning out to be her worst one yet.

Her parents' house seemed smaller, confining, now that she had to share it with Keith. The man that had betrayed her in more ways than one. She directed her attention towards him, narrowing her eyes as if squinting would help her to see all his flaws. Maybe a few minutes of observation would put what was going on into some perspective she could understand.

Joshua slouched on the floor in front of her chair. "Are you being my protector?" She placed her hand on her brother's shoulder, happy to have him so close.

"I've got your back." He turned just enough to give her his winning smile.

"So now what? Are we supposed to sit here and pretend that everything okay?" Bliss stared at Keith, then Marc, who was seated on the sofa. He too was a reasonable distance from Keith. Did everyone feel the need to put a little more space between them and Keith? His confessional note had placed the spotlight on him and the revelation wasn't too pretty.

Her stomach twisted into a tight knot and threatened to force her lunch back up.

"This was never about you, Bliss. I didn't want to get you involved and I made sure that everyone who asked me understood that you weren't involved. I didn't know what else to do." There was probably enough sadness in Keith's voice to convince everyone else in the room that he was worthy of their empathy, but she'd seen this act before. She'd heard the same tone when he swore she was paranoid and Megan was only a friend. And the same timbre dripped from his lips when he forgot her birthday.

She pushed back against the chair and crossed her arms over her chest. "It looks like your convincing didn't work. Roger told me this morning the investigators want to talk to me." She bit her lip and pointed her index finger at him. "I swear, Keith, if this thing goes sour--"

"Nothing is going to happen to you. I'll see to it."

"Huh. I can't believe you did this. I just don't understand." She continued to stare at him.

Marc held up his hand. "We don't have to do anything for a while. It's snowing. We're stuck here. Let's just make the best of things."

She directed her gaze at Keith. "Were you really thinking about killing yourself, or was it an attempt for sympathy?"

His eyes went dead.

"I'm sorry. It's just hard to know when you're being truthful and when you're manipulating a situation." She rubbed her eyes with her finger-tips. "Maybe right now I should just keep my mouth shut. I don't know what to think or what to say."

Marc jumped up. "I tell you what, Joshua why don't you keep Keith company while Bliss and I go in the kitchen." He nodded toward the door. "And see what we can come up with for dinner."

"Good idea." She unfolded her legs and left the room before Marc.

In the kitchen, she pulled the food items from the boxes that Marc had placed on the counter. Christmas Eve dinner was tomorrow night and she wasn't any closer to getting a grasp on things than she was when she accepted the responsibilities her father had placed on her.

Marc walked into the kitchen with the self-assuredness of a man watching a disaster unfold that didn't involve him. His no-wrinkle khaki and thick wool sweater didn't wear the ruins of the day like her cotton chinos that were now wrinkled and smeared with her foundation and some black soot she must have picked up from the car. Marc was about as unflappable as James Bond. That's what she needed in her life. A man that was rock solid, not one who would stage a suicide and implicate his girlfriend to go down with him.

"I can't believe what is happening here." She threw her arms up. "I feel like I've stepped out of my life and into some poorly written soap opera."

"Are you okay?" Marc came up behind her and placed his warm hands on her shoulders. The gentle massage did nothing to relieve the tension in her shoulders and neck.

"Harder." She could only manage a whisper. "Press harder."

He stepped closer and increased the pressure. She could feel the heat emanating from his body. The chill buried in her bones warmed. Without meaning to, she relaxed against him. For a moment she didn't want to think about the list of things she needed to do or how Keith had betrayed her or how he might have jeopardized her job. She gave her body permission to relax and take the pleasure that Marc offered. For a few moments, she didn't want to be the glue that held everything together. She wanted to put her wants in front of everyone and everything else. Why not? Wasn't she entitled to that every now and then? What would happen? The world wouldn't stop spinning. Christmas would still come. Keith would still be a lair. And Marc... She didn't know about Marc. And for now, that was okay. If he was around for a few more minutes or a few more days, she'd enjoy whatever he was willing to share.

He teased a knot at the base of her neck. The painful, pleasurable sensation made staying straight up difficult. This kind of treatment deserved a darkened room, soft sheets, and mellow music. Instead, she had the garish lights of the kitchen, a counter full of packaged foods, and her ex-boyfriend just a few feet away.

To move from the past and into the present, she had to take control of her life, of what she wanted and what she wanted to do. She spun around to face him and dropped her arms over his head and around his neck. He hesitated for a moment before sliding his tongue into her mouth and pressing his solid chest into her.

What started out as a passionate kiss deepened into one of those kisses that made her want to shed underwear and spread her legs. But she couldn't do either, right now. Marc ended the kiss and inhaled a deep breath. He held her at arm's length and stared into her eyes like he was searching for answers. "What's going on here, Bliss?"

She rolled her tingling lips together. "What do you mean?"

"Your ex-boyfriend is sitting in your parent's living room, just minutes after we have sex." He shook his head. "You have to know I haven't been hanging around because I don't have anything else to do? You can't be that naive."

She shifted positions, dodging his words. This straightforwardness was new. Where were the words of dance where he almost said what he wanted and she pretended to be interested just a little? Had maturity taught him how to ask for what he wanted instead of hoping that someone's instincts would kick in and grant him his wish?

"Keith is not my boyfriend. He might have broken up with me a few days ago, but we parted ways a long time ago." She clasped her hands. Her holiday manicure was already chipping.

Marc reached for her hands and held them for a moment. "I'm not putting any pressure on you. I just want to be clear with you and I need you to be honest and upfront with me."

"I don't know if I know how."

"It's easier than you think. You can tell me what you're feeling and what you're thinking. There are no right or wrong answers."

She closed her eyes and took her time opening them. "I don't know what kind of psycho-babble you're peddling. Telling someone what's really on my mind has only gotten me into trouble. If I could say what I want, then Keith would not be sitting in my parent's living room. I feel like I need to be sympathetic because he might be suicidal. But that's not what I'm feeling in my heart. Does that make me a bad person?"

"No. You feel what you feel. There is no way that can be wrong."

She exhaled out of her mouth. "I shouldn't need validation for my feelings, but thank you. Keith means nothing to me. I'll be nice until he can get back on the road. And as for us, well, I am hoping you will be sticking around because you like my long legs and big brown eyes."

"Believe me there's more of you to like than your legs and eyes. He adjusted his pants and shook his legs. "I think we were supposed to be finding something in here to eat."

"Yeah, right." She looked away. "We can pull some stuff together, but I don't think anyone has an appetite. I know I don't."

"So, whatever we make won't matter. The sooner we get this part over the sooner we can get back to us."

He waved his finger at himself, then at her in that cool way that teens do and all she wanted to do was kiss him again.

Chapter Seven

Marc glanced around. The remnants of the thrown together dinner still cluttered the table. Bliss's prediction was right. No one had much of an appetite and even less desire to talk. Instead of a merry-go-round of sparkling conversation, they'd sat at the table staring at the food and pretending not to notice how fidgety Keith was. He couldn't stop looking at Bliss.

For a man who had managed his life detail by detail, Marc struggled with managing his emotions. The age gap was a big deal. The distance between Manhattan and Wilmington was a big deal. Her addiction to work and his laid-back approach to life was a big deal. Bigger than their age difference.

What was he thinking, making love to her? She wasn't just some woman. He was never careless. He forced down a final forkful of chicken salad. The last taste wasn't as good as the first. Doubt crept into the fringes of his thoughts. He could almost see the shadows whose only plan was to coat his life in guilt. He was supposed to mourn the memory of his dead wife forever, not enjoy an amazing tussle in the sheets with a woman thirteen-years his junior, who couldn't be serious about him. The age difference had to register with her.

He pushed away from the table. This always happened. Whenever he developed feelings for someone, the urge to run swarmed him. Wanting to be with someone else didn't seem right.

Looking out the window in the living room, he shoved his hands into his pockets. "The snow has stopped," he called over his shoulder to the others. Which meant this was a perfect time for him to make his escape or for Keith to make his.

No one responded.

"Did you guys hear me? Soon the roads will be clear. We won't be stuck here anymore." He spoke louder.

Bliss came to stand behind him. "If snow plow drivers are anything like they used to be, they will be here soon. We'll hear them, I'm sure." She encircled his waist with her arms. "You're not in a hurry to get away, are you?"

"Not at all." What else could he say? He couldn't say he was losing the ability to breathe or that this much domestication was suffocating him or that he needed the quiet of his own house to sort out his emotions. How could one compact beauty make his life so complicated?

He kissed her forehead, not caring if Keith saw the gesture. "I will need to get to my house some time tonight or first thing in the morning. I have to get some edits completed and sent to my editor."

She dropped her arms. "Good to know you don't live completely off the grid. A man with some deadlines—I was beginning to worry that you weren't human."

Joshua entered the room with Keith at his side. "So, what's up sis? Are we supposed to just sit around all night? I'm not into board games." He looked around the room. "I have plans for this evening which did not include any of this." He waved his hand around the room.

"Why don't we decorate the tree?" Marc asked. "That's another thing you can scratch off your list and right now you have plenty of help." As long as he was busy, thoughts of Bliss, mixed with Rachel, and the holidays wouldn't drag him down.

####

Bliss opened a box of gold ornaments shaped like teardrops. These were her favorite. As a child, she'd always hung these from the low branches of the tree. She was still giddy from the few moments shared with Marc before Keith and Joshua descended on the house. She couldn't help evaluating their motives for sleeping together. Was the incident just a fauxlationship?

They weren't committed to each other.

They hardly knew each other.

She'd even forgotten to ask him if he was seeing someone.

Was he into men and when was the last time he was tested for STD's?

She'd been so distracted, she'd forgotten her core questions she always asked before getting too involved.

Decorating the tree—the activity that should have been festive didn't come close. Joshua leaned on the wall near the door staring at his phone. Hoping for the great escape, no doubt. Keith sat in the chair. With his head hung down, it was hard to tell what was on his mind. Marc was the only one who'd grabbed a box of tree decorations to help her. He was different now. She couldn't say just how, but he wasn't fully present. Maybe the chaos that had unfolded was now dragging him under. There was an emptiness in his eyes that hadn't been there a few hours ago.

Bliss placed her box of tree bulbs on the table. Now was the time to clear the house. Maybe this was the time for Marc to take his leave, too. But she was going to start with the most unwanted person in the room.

"Keith, can I talk to you in the kitchen for a moment?"

He lifted his head. His ashen coloring didn't do much to alleviate her worry over his mental health.

He pushed out of the chair and followed her without commenting.

At the island in the kitchen, she motioned to the chair. "Are you alright?"

He stared at her. His face unmoving.

"I know that's a silly question, but what I mean is—are you, were you really going to kill yourself? You can be honest. This is just between you and me."

He ran his hand down his face. "Yes. No. I thought I could. I just want to stop worrying about this stuff. What's going to happen? But no. I couldn't. I can't think straight. I don't know what to do." He dropped his head into his hands.

"Yes, you do. You know what you need to do. You just don't want to do it."

"Suppose I go to jail?" He spoke into the palms of his hands.

"Talk to a lawyer. Maybe you can cut some kind of deal. You need to contact someone before you're arrested. The company will find out, so get ahead of this before you have no options."

"Will you come back to New York with me? I don't want to do this alone."

"I'm not going back to New York until after the holidays."

She closed her eyes for a moment. How selfish could one man be? He was the definition of self-helpless. She could see his picture next to the words as if they were in the dictionary. Her mother was in the hospital. Christmas was days away and he wanted to drag her back to New York to handle his drama. She shook her head. "Keith, you need to do this on your own."

"Are you kicking me out?"

She wanted to say yes. To get this thing with Keith over, so she could move on with her life. As long as he was here, she was stuck in the middle of a vast plane of nothing. But putting him out in the midst of a blizzard, right before Christmas wasn't in her heart either. Somehow she and Keith would get through the holidays. She wasn't sure how she'd explain his being here to everyone, but there was enough time to worry about explanations later.

She touched his arm. "No. I'm not kicking you out. I just want to make sure we're in agreement on what's happening. We are not a couple. We're friends. Understood?" The strings between them needed to be severed and this was the time. She wanted to forget old acquaintances and get more familiar with new ones, like Marc, whose character ran deeper than the clothes he wore or the restaurants he took to her for dinner.

"You're into that old dude, aren't you? I don't know how to compete with him. I didn't know you were looking for a father figure."

She chuckled. "Have you seen my father? Marc is nothing at all like my father, but that has nothing to do with you and me. We both know we haven't really been in a relationship in a long time. You used me because you didn't want to be alone. And I let you because I was too busy at work to do what needed to be done."

The helplessness in his eyes was overwhelming, but she couldn't give in to him. He was left over from a time in her life that she wanted to move beyond. Back when she was willing to accept far less than she deserved.

Chapter Eight

Bliss remained seated in the kitchen. Confrontation may be easy for some people, but not for her. Letting Keith sit in the living room, studying his hands while they all moved on to live normal lives would have been her option of choice. Her father would get around to telling him he had to leave at some point.

She could hear Keith paraphrasing their conversation. As if he'd been the one to make some final decisions about their relationship. Correcting him wasn't worth the effort. There were a few low murmurs, but she forced her butt to stay put. Keith would work things out for himself. If he couldn't, there wasn't a thing more she could do for him.

The front door opened. The house was quiet. She stood but waited a minute longer before checking the living room. Outside she could see the three of them digging the cars out of the snow. Marc and Joshua did all the work. Keith's movements were half-hearted.

"He'll find his way," she whispered.

She turned her attention to the tree. Except for her box of ornaments, the tree was complete. With a deep sigh, she shouldered her purse before taking the stairs to her bedroom two at a time.

She couldn't let go of the bothersome thought of why Marc was doing so much to help her. Understanding her emotions was easy. She'd had a crush on him for years, even though it had settled into the background of her life. But the moment she saw him, the awareness had assailed her again. This wasn't the time to question her good fortune. This was the time to just enjoy him.

What she needed was a few moments alone, to work on the report. She pulled her phone from her purse. There were six messages. All of which needed to be returned.

The thin band of hope that she could get everything done was fading quicker than the setting sun. She turned on her computer, found the report, and started in. The only time she didn't question her ability was with work.

Numbers she understood.

Sales projections she understood.

Office politics she understood.

There were no questions about which task to do first or if she was doing them right. Unlike in her personal relationships with women and men, where she wondered if she should call first, or if she was calling too much, or if she'd said the right things, or done the right things. To her, the time spent doing self-examination on her personal life was exhausting.

An hour later, footsteps on the stairs warned her that someone was coming to invade on her time. Joshua was keeping a little distance, just in case she asked for the money he owed her. That left Marc or Keith.

Marc stuck his head in the room. "I should have known the moment you were left alone, you'd take off to your computer or your phone."

"I needed to get some work done and thought this was the perfect time." She pressed the save button on her computer.

"Keith told us you invited him to stay through the holidays." There was a catch in his voice. Was he jealous?

"I don't feel like I had much choice. He wasn't invited, exactly. He's like the uncle that just won't go home and doesn't bathe every day." She exhaled and fell against the headboard.

He came into the room. "Your brother left."

"I'm sure he did. That little sneak."

"What's so sneaky about leaving?"

"He owes me money. Money that he probably has no intention of paying back, or will pay back months from now when he's good and ready."

"How much?"

"I won't take money from you, so don't ask. This is between me and my brother." She pushed a lock of hair behind her ear. "Tell me something, Marc?" She stared down at her hands still positioned on the keyboard. "Why have you been so nice to me? Doing all this stuff. Tell me what's in this for you?"

He exhaled through his mouth. He plopped on the bed. "I wish I could give you a definitive answer. At the train station, you looked like you needed help. After spending time with you, I couldn't pull myself away. You're like a magnet. I keep saying I'm going to go home, but then something happens."

She claimed his mouth. They didn't need to talk anymore. He'd said all the right things. Since Keith and Joshua had shown up, that's all they had done was talk. If he was getting ready to leave she wanted another few luscious moments of nothing but him.

Marc stood up. "I'm going to leave." He wiped his mouth. "I've got some stuff I need to take care of." Even though he didn't sound like he was trying to get away from her, something close to dread crawled up her spine and settled in her stomach. Why had he wiped his mouth after her kiss?

"I see." She managed. "I need to start prepping for tomorrow's dinner anyway."

"Can you cook? Have you ever cooked a big meal?"

"No. I'm going to find my mother's recipes. I can read and follow instructions, so how hard can cooking be?"

He leaned his head back. The throaty laughter was a happy sound. "I'd like to be there when you take a bite of your first dish."

She swatted him. "Oh, I was planning on you being here. You'll come to dinner, won't you? And since you're so good at criticizing, maybe you can help me." The comment was a cheesy way to get him to come back. She wasn't ready to let him walk away. Maybe if they tried and put in a good effort, they could turn whatever this was into something special.

####

Marc backed out of the Duncan's family driveway. With the car in first gear, he made his way up the icy hill. He cracked the window in the car to allow the frigid air to sting his face. Something was needed to pull him out of the funk he was in. Somehow, he'd managed five whole years without having some woman come along and upend his world. Then there was Bliss.

What was he thinking? Dating someone so much younger was bound to be problematic. An old boyfriend hanging around for the holidays wasn't normal. Maybe she and Keith had the kind of relationship where they faded in and out—breaking up and getting back together. Maybe Keith was back, for now.

He needed to stay away from her. He couldn't risk getting his heart broken, just when it was beginning to heal. She'd go back to New York. He'd go back to his office next to his bedroom. She'd find someone her own age to date—maybe Keith or someone else. He'd go back to dating faceless women to fill the boredom when it struck.

He nodded. At least now he had a plan. Even if he wasn't so sure he liked it.

Snow was falling again. The fine flakes drifted around much like he was today. Finally reaching his house, he turned off the car. Until the driveway was cleared he'd have to park here. Instead of going into his house, he knocked on his neighbor's door.

"Marc, hello." Lucy swung the door wide open. Bugsy, their cocker spaniel, charged toward him. Marc reached down to pet the dog. "Floyd and I were just getting ready to trim our tree. Come on in. You can have a glass of Merlot and be our mediator when Floyd tries to put the blue ornaments on the tree."

The tautness in his shoulders gave him a reprieve. He was back amongst his kind of people. Lucy and Floyd were his age. They knew Rachel. The two of them were always encouraging him to move on. What would they say if they knew he wanted to move on with someone like Bliss?

"Where you been all day, buddy? With that cute chick we saw you with at the tree lot?" Floyd slapped him on the back. "Bugsy missed you. I actually had to take him for his afternoon walk." He handed a glass of Merlot to Marc.

"I've been tied up. I'll make it up to Bugsy tomorrow." He flopped on the sofa.

"So, what was her name again?" Lucy asked. Marc could almost see the barrage of questions gathering in her head. She was so much like Rachel. No wonder they were best friends.

"Why do you think I was tied up with her?" Marc averted his glance.

"You can't get anything past Lucy. I swear my wife has a sixth and a seventh sense. You might as well come clean. She won't give you any peace until you do." Floyd picked up the box of blue ornaments.

"Put that box down, Floyd. We're not going with blue this year." Lucy sat beside Marc. "What's going on?"

He shook his head. "I just ran into her. She used to be a student. She needed my help today." He took a swallow of the Merlot. What he needed was a shot of Scotch. Double Malt.

"If that's all there was, then why are you acting so squirrelly?" She pointed her index finger at him. "You like her, don't you?"

"Lucy, I was helping someone in need." Marc insisted. "She's years younger than me."

"So what." Lucy batted his comment aside.

"I think she's more interested in her career then she is in a relationship." He swirled the dark liquid around in his glass. "I'm not willing to go through that again."

Lucy squeezed his knee. "Just because she's a hard worker, that doesn't mean she's compulsive like Rachel."

"I'm not sure I want to take that chance." He shrugged. "Besides, we're not that far yet anyway." Saying the words wasn't the same as believing them, but in time he would. Packing up his emotions and keeping them locked away was something he knew how to do.

"Leave the man alone, Lucy. Can't you see he doesn't want to talk," Floyd said.

"There is nothing to talk about." Marc stood. "I ran into her the day before yesterday. Helped her out today. There is nothing else to tell."

Lucy's eyes widened. "You had sex." She made the statement without any judgment. She could have been talking about the snow. "No, let me correct that. You made love this time." She looked over at her husband. "He made love, Floyd." She almost sang the words.

Floyd shook his head. "You see why I will never cheat. She'd know before I even got back home."

"Lucy, I don't want to talk about this right now. Just decorate your tree and let me enjoy your wine."

Lucy pushed off the sofa. She removed the blue ornaments that Floyd had placed on the tree. "Are you coming to dinner on Christmas? I'm making some of your favorites."

He drained his glass. "I've been here every year since..." He took a breath. "Yeah, I'll be here. Where else would I go?"

Chapter Nine

Bliss stood in the kitchen. Christmas Eve had arrived a little too soon. The counters were cluttered with all the fixings for making the dinner staples. Viewing several YouTube videos overnight, had made this cooking thing sound easy enough. She propped her tablet on the counter to watch the video again.

"I knew you could do this, baby." Her father hurried in the kitchen. "The Christmas tree is perfect. Did you wrap all those gifts yourself?" He reached for a cup from the cabinet.

"You really didn't think Joshua was going to help me, did you?" She poured coffee for her father. "I will give him credit for clearing the snow in the driveway and he may have hung a bulb on the tree." She placed the turkey in the sink. With a gloved hand, she reached into the cavity to remove the giblets and neck.

Her father snickered. "He's going through some stuff. Cut him a break." He took the seat at the counter. "Tell me again who's sleeping in the other room upstairs. He's your friend, but not your boyfriend?"

"We're not a couple, Dad. He's just having some trouble so I'm letting him spend the holidays with us."

"You like this guy?"

"No. Not like that. We're friends." She placed the innards in a bowl and ran water inside the bird.

"What kind of trouble? It's not drugs, is it?"

She faced her father. "Dad, no, we're not talking street drugs. He's having some issues at work. Please don't worry. He'll be going home right after the holiday. Now please tell me you spoke with the aunts and they're bringing the side dishes?"

"Yep, they are. And I'd better get out of here to pick up your mother. After being in the hospital the last few days, she is anxious to get home." He stood. "Where's that fellow, Marc?"

"He's coming to dinner." She hoped. He hadn't picked up last night when she called. She tried to ignore the emptiness swelling in her chest. She couldn't be in love with Marc, could she? Was the rumbling in her stomach what all her friends swooned about? Was it love? Whatever was going on between them was greater than anything she'd felt before.

She waved her father goodbye, then pulled off the large yellow gloves.

Keith strolled into the kitchen dressed as if he was on his way to meet the Queen of England. She glanced down at her sweater pants, bare feet, and shook her head. What had she ever seen in him?

"What's for breakfast?" He took the seat her father had just vacated.

"Are you kidding me? You cannot, absolutely cannot, be that self-centered. I just had my arm stuck up a turkey and you think I want to cook you breakfast?"

"I just thought—"

"No, you didn't. That's just it, you don't think of anyone but yourself." She pulled cereal from the pantry and slammed the box down in front of him. "Help yourself. There is milk in the refrigerator. Use the carton with the 'J' on it."

She left Keith seated at the counter. Putting some space between the two of them probably saved him from being choked this morning. A twenty-two-pound turkey needed to be stuffed. Two pounds of string beans needed to be cooked, and there was a five-pound bag of potatoes waiting for her to peel. "Hey Keith, do you know how to peel potatoes?" She called from the living room.

"How hard can it be? I've seen my mother do it a hundred times."

"Good. Can you peel that bag at the end of the counter? Just put them in cold water when you're done. I'll be right back." She charged up the stairs. In the security of her bedroom, she closed the door.

She dialed Marc's phone. For someone who'd seemed more than interested in her a few days ago, why hadn't he returned her call? She hung up. This time she was going to be different. For once, this once, why couldn't she be the one pursued? Again, relationship intricacies had bested her. What hint had she missed?

She sat on the edge of the bed. The room was back to normal. No gifts waiting to be wrapped. The scent of Marc had faded sometime yesterday evening. The only thing that lingered were her memories.

The way he'd touched her.

The way he'd tasted her.

The way he'd said her name in that moment.

He was as distant to her now as he was at the University. The feeling of being foolish for thinking she could be anything to him wouldn't stop poking at her.

Focusing on what she was good at might help to ease the heaviness sitting on her chest. While her computer booted up she stared at her ring finger. She hadn't been one of those girls who planned her wedding or named her children before she met someone, but she'd gotten her hopes up with Marc. Again. If Christmas was supposed to be that special time of year, why couldn't it be special for her too? This year she'd gotten several early gifts and all of them resembled coal.

An hour later, she made her way back to the kitchen. Keith was still at the sink with the biggest knife in the house.

"I thought you said you knew how to peel potatoes." She glanced down in the sink.

"I do."

She reached in the drawer for a paring knife. "You've done a pretty good job of butchering the potatoes. I just hope we have enough left to feed everyone."

"I tell you what, if I notice there isn't enough, I won't eat any." Keith grinned. The first time since he showed up.

"Let me finish up in here. I need to get the stuffing made and the turkey in the oven if we're going to eat dinner at six. Why don't you go turn on the television and watch a ballgame? My mother should be home soon."

Keith put his knife down. Within seconds he was out of the kitchen. Leaving her alone to stew in the mess she'd created.

####

Marc stared at his reflection in the entry hall mirror. He looked like himself. He recognized the salt and pepper hair, the nose that slanted a little too much to the left. But something was going on inside of his head that wasn't recognizable. Something he had no problem avoiding until now.

Bliss had called last night and again this morning. But what could he say to her? He dragged his hand down his face. There was no use in pretending he wasn't going to show up at her place for dinner. He would. Not taking her calls was the hardest thing he had to do in years. But going any further would be devastating. Was he ready to leave Rachel behind?

After Rachel's death, he'd avoided anything that required too much thought, too much energy and too much of him. And Bliss deserved nothing less. He couldn't half-ass it with her.

"Damn her." He muttered. He'd been so transparent Lucy read him like a well-used deck of tarot cards. But he knew what he had to do.

With his car keys clutched in the palm of his hand, he made his way to the car.

Lucy was in the yard with Bugsy. "Hey, Marc, where you headed?"

If only he'd left a few minutes sooner or later, he could have gotten away from her interrogation. "To dinner." He tried to sound casual enough to quash any more questions from her.

"On Christmas Eve?" She dropped the leash to make her way towards him. Her footsteps crunched in the high snow. She had to take long awkward strides to reach him. "You haven't been out on Christmas Eve since..." She paused for a second. "This woman must be pretty special. Please try to bring her by tomorrow for dinner if she doesn't have plans."

"No." He shook his head. "I'm sure she's going to have dinner with her family." Telling Lucy too much was a fatal mistake. Lucy would still be talking about Bliss long after Bliss was back in New York dating someone new and long after he'd moved on to safe ground with some faceless woman.

"At least ask her. Maybe she could come by later for drinks. I'd like to see her again."

"You're just being nosy. You want to see if she meets your approval." Marc shoved his hands in the pocket of his coat.

"I'm looking out for you." She reached out and rubbed his sleeve. "I promised I would."

"I'm a big boy, Lucy. I'm not in a relationship, so don't get your hopes up. She is no different than the other ones." He opened the door to the car. Denying Bliss was a betrayal of his emotions, but caring for her was a betrayal of Rachel. There was no way out for him.

Lucy pointed her finger at him. "You're lying and I know you are. You didn't die, Rachel did. Stop acting like you've been sentenced to a life all alone. She doesn't want you to mourn forever."

"How do you know that, Lucy? How can you be so sure of what Rachel wanted for me?" He didn't mean to raise his voice but the ache in his chest wouldn't let go. He climbed into the car and closed the door.

Lucy tapped on the car window. She was persistent. That was one of the things he loved and hated about her.

He put the window down. "Yes."

"Because Rachel told me. She told me to make sure you didn't." There were tears in her eyes. Big, fat tears like she'd just spoken to Rachel.

Chapter Ten

When Bliss first arrived home, Christmas Eve seemed like it was eons away. So much had happened in such a short period of time, thinking about everything made her gulp for air. She'd pulled off her mother's request. That accomplishment should have been enough to buoy her for months. But something else was brewing. Even though she didn't know what was coming, she had a feeling she wasn't going to like it.

She placed the last dish on the table. The spread didn't look as appetizing as something her mother would have done, but she'd done pretty well for a rookie. In two days, she could go back to New York, forget about Marc and bury herself in her work.

In something she knew.

Where the rules were written in ink.

Where she could concentrate on things she could control.

Her father came up beside her. "This looks good, baby girl." He placed his hand on her shoulder. "Have you seen your mother's face? She hasn't stopped smiling since she walked through the door."

"I just hope everything tastes as good as it looks. I'm not the cook she is, but let's hope I make a decent stand-in."

He nodded to the living room. "From the laughter coming from in there, I think everyone is enjoying themselves. Your Aunt put so much brandy in the eggnog, everything will taste good."

"Did you invite your new friend to dinner?"

She hesitated for a moment. Her new friend. Is that how she wanted to label Marc--a friend? If only she felt as casual as the word sounded. "Yeah, but he wasn't sure if he was going to be able to come."

"From the way he looked at you, I think he's more than a little interested."

She shook her head. If that was true, it would be wonderful, but the two of them were opposites, just like her and Keith. And that relationship was one big disaster. "Marc has been very nice. I couldn't have made this happen without his help." She kept her voice level.

Her father gave her the same smile he'd given her as a child when he tried to encourage her to try her bicycle without the training wheels. "I know more than you're giving me credit for. I've seen you two together. The two of you remind me of your mother and me."

"Dad, I think you've had too much eggnog."

"Yeah, but this time is different." With his hand on her back, he guided her into the living room.

Marc was standing next to the fireplace. He locked eyes with her for a moment. There was something unspoken that passed between them. But instead of the warm sensation she'd had two days ago, this time her stomach knotted. He blinked a moment too soon which was never a good thing.

Why hadn't he sought her out when he arrived? His posture spoke to his level of comfort with her family. His elbow was positioned on the fireplace. A glass of eggnog in his hand. Keith, on the other hand looked like he'd rather chew on rocks than talk with her family. Compared to Marc, everything about Keith was immature and lacking. As different as they were, one of them should have been right for her. But no. When it came to men, her picker was broken.

The serious look on Marc's face disappeared, softening into the kind of expression she'd gotten used to. He crossed the room, making his way toward her. She forced air out of her lungs.

"Hey." He kissed her on the cheek. A warm sensation traveled along her spine. Would every time be like this, or was this only happening because of the newness of their relationship? Like a toy they hadn't grown bored of and tossed aside.

"I wasn't sure you'd come." She examined his face. Would his eyes tell her something his words wouldn't? "I called you several times."

"I know."

She bit back the question she wanted to ask. At least he hadn't pretended he didn't get the calls. This wasn't the time to have this discussion with him. For a few more moments, the joy of everything she'd accomplished today needed to be enjoyed. Besides, everyone in the room had stopped talking and had turned their attention on her.

"Dinner is ready. Let's eat." She waved her arms to the dining room. The need to put some space between her and Marc overwhelmed her. What was there to say? They weren't a couple. They had only shared a few moments together. A Christmas fling. Tomorrow afternoon, she was going to be back in New York and he was going to be doing whatever he usually did on Christmas evening. She'd find a way to accept what they had. All she had to do now was stay away from him to avoid the awkward conversation. The one that ended with I'll call you or we'll always be friends or you're very special to me. None of those tired lines would make her feel better.

Three glasses of eggnog had dulled her senses. With each guest that left the anxiety in her stomach eased enough for her to breathe without struggling.

Marc pushed his shoulder into hers. "I'm going to leave now. Give you some time to spend with your family."

She faked a smile. "Let me walk you to the door."

"No need. Stay here." He placed his hand on her thigh. The pressure he applied kept her in the chair. "Dinner was delicious. We'll talk tomorrow."

"Sure," she croaked.

He pushed away from the table and moments later, she heard the front door close. He'd be surprised when he tried to reach her tomorrow. The moment she left Delaware, she was leaving him also.

After everyone was gone, Bliss put the last dish in the dishwasher. The kitchen was clean, her feet ached, and the house was finally quiet, except for Joshua and his wife. She'd asked him to keep Keith entertained until she was done.

As long as she stayed in the kitchen, she didn't have to worry that someone would ask questions about Marc. Because she didn't have any answers for them or herself.

Joshua came into the kitchen. "So, what is going on with you and the professor? That relationship didn't last long."

"We didn't have a relationship, Joshua." She dried her hands on the towel without looking at her brother.

"Isn't that what I just said?" He snickered.

"Go to hell."

"Oh, don't take me so seriously. I was only joking with you. Anyway, you've still got Keith. He looks a little less fidgety today."

She walked closer to her brother. "Well, let's hope he can hold himself together when we get back to New York tomorrow. That's when his ass is going to get a good kick."

Joshua dropped his arm around her shoulder. "I've got your money." He pulled a check from his pocket. "I'm sorry. I know I should have repaid you earlier, but..."

She touched his hand. "I knew you would. But when was the question. Keith purchased me a train ticket home to thank me and I don't have a Christmas gift for you." She shrugged a shoulder.

"You can give it to me later." He kissed her cheek. "And sorry things didn't work out with the professor. I kinda liked him."

She rubbed her brother's arm. If she tried to speak, the words would stick in her throat. Instead, she nodded. Putting her feelings for Marc into words was impossible. Marc had opened a door long enough for her to see inside to the possibility of love. To feel the lightheaded, bubbly feeling that she'd seen in movies.

She wanted that with someone.

With Marc.

Chapter Eleven

Marc stood at his front door. Christmas morning felt like every other day of the year, except for the falling snow. The twinkle lights on almost every house on the block were another giveaway. A white Christmas. For the first time since he could remember.

Maybe Bliss's mother was right, there was magic in the holidays. Or a sense of well-being. There was only one flaw in the holidays for him. He didn't believe in magic. If such a thing existed, he wouldn't be standing in his house trying to think of a reason not to visit his neighbor for Christmas dinner. Or he wouldn't have gotten involved with Bliss. The hurt in her eyes yesterday was a solid blow to his heart. Better to hurt her now than wait until they both were too far in.

He pulled his phone from his pants pocket to dial her number for the second time within hours. She wasn't picking up and she wouldn't this time, either. The phone rang four times before going to her voice mail. Her actions were purposeful. She always had her phone within inches of her fingers. He deserved as much. Hadn't he ignored her calls the other night?

What was she doing this morning? Enjoying her mother's return home. Laughing with her family. Maybe she was relishing the smug feeling of having laid the college professor and now she was ready to get on with her real life. Conquest accomplished. Either way, he'd cherish every moment he'd spent with her. For a few days, he'd been happy. Like he used to be when laughter came easy.

He picked up the cup of coffee off the entrance table. The reheated brew from last night was bitter, but he swallowed it anyway. The taste matched his mood.

What he needed was an excuse to get out of going to dinner next door. Hearing Lucy's evaluation of his life was unnecessary. He already knew everything she was going to say. On the outside, he looked like an ordinary man. One capable of conquering the irrational thoughts of a man dealing with the ghost of his dead wife. But on the inside, he was as torn up as he'd been five years ago. Unable to make any progress. With Bliss, he thought he could. Bliss was the first time the possibility seemed within his reach. But the dark cloud had found him and coated him in that familiar darkness he'd grown used to.

From the window in the door, he could see Floyd in the yard with Bugsy. Cars were lined up in their driveway. All of their guests had probably arrived. If he tried to back out now, Lucy would don her superhero cape and try to rescue him. Marc sighed before squaring his shoulders.

He hurried across the lawn. Without his coat, the frigid temperature cut through his thin shirt.

"I was beginning to think you weren't coming. Lucy told me she grilled you pretty hard yesterday, so I couldn't blame you." Floyd headed back inside behind the dog. He held the door for Marc.

"Let's hope she gives me a break today."

"Don't count on it. She thinks her duty is to make sure you're happy. She's turned it into her life's mission."

Marc reached down to pet Bugsy. "Maybe with all her family here she won't have time to focus on me today."

Floyd slapped him on the back. "You can wish."

Marc wiped his feet on the rug. Some college bowl game blared from the television. He made his way to the bar Floyd always set up near the television. That way no one had to miss a play while fixing their drink.

He found an empty folding chair in the corner and settled in. Two family gatherings in two days. For a man with very little family, the oddity of the idea made him chuckle. Next year, he'd opt for a sunny island. He'd welcome Christmas morning with his feet buried in the sand and a drink with a paper umbrella floating on top.

By the time Lucy announced dinner was ready, he was still nursing his first drink. Yesterday's eggnog still had his head hungover.

Lucy's table was twice the size of the one at the Duncan house, which meant there were twice as many people. Floyd sat at one end of the table and Lucy sat next to him. Marc took a seat at the opposite end. Lucy didn't seem to take any special notice of him. In another hour he could slink back to his place and wait out the rest of the holidays.

"Hello, Marc."

He looked up. Lucy's co-worker slid into the seat next to him. Certain she'd seen the wince he couldn't control, he tried to make nice. "Hello." He searched for her name. "Amy, right?"

"Audrey," she said. "I see Lucy still gets you to come to the dinner for the misfit friends. I was hoping to get out of it this year but...here I am. She sprinkles us in with her family and thinks we don't notice the charity." Audrey threw up her hands.

"I think the trick to avoiding this pitfall is to plan well in advance. Like starting tomorrow."

She snapped her fingers. "I'll do that. I know her intentions are good, but just because I'm alone doesn't mean I need to be extricated from myself. I'm fine with a frozen dinner and watching old movies on Christmas day."

Marc glanced down the table at Floyd and Lucy. The two of them were leaning into each other, whispering, then Floyd kissed her on the forehead. Marc wanted to look away. He felt like a peeping-tom watching an intimate moment, the foreplay before the sex, but he couldn't. The genuine happiness shared by the two of them was contagious. Their happiness infected everyone around them. So, if he sat long enough maybe some would get on him.

"Yeah, look at the two of them," Audrey nodded to the opposite end of the table. "When you have something that special, I guess you can't help wanting it for everyone else, too."

Marc turned his attention to his empty plate. "I guess you're right." He reached for the platter of roast beef.

Were Lucy and Floyd happy because the gods had looked down on them and granted them something special? Or were they happy because they pushed past all the obstacles and persevered in the face of everything that challenged them?

After dinner, Lucy cornered him before he could get back to the safety of his house. "Did you invite your friend to dinner?"

He looked at the door, his only escape route. "No, she had plans."

"You didn't even ask her, did you?"

"How do you know so much? Has it ever occurred to you that you could be wrong about something?" He kept his voice low.

"Almost, once." She smiled before slipping her arm through his. She led him into her small office adjacent to the living room. Another ball game was playing. He'd almost gotten free. But after the big meal, he was moving slow. Easy prey.

"What do you want from me, Lucy? What can I say to get you to leave me alone for the rest of the day?"

"Don't say anything. Let me do the talking." She placed one hand on the side of his face. The smell of her cologne fought with the smell of sage.

"Okay. But if I listen, then you have to cease and desist for at least three months."

She dropped her hand to his leg. From any other woman, the act would have been sensual, with Lucy it was concern. "I saw you checking your phone all through dinner. What did you do to screw up this time?"

He fell against the love seat. "Do you know how annoying you can be? Nobody likes a know-it-all."

The warm smile she gave him let him know he hadn't hurt her feelings. "Stop being afraid, Marc."

"Why do you think I'm afraid? I'm not afraid of anything."

"Don't you sound just like a man? Put your ego back in your pants and listen to me," she paused. "You loved Rachel, right?"

He looked down at his hands.

"If you would have known in advance she was going to die, would you have skipped over her?"

"Of course not." He straightened and pulled away from Lucy. "How could you ask me such an appalling question?"

"That's my point. Love any way you can experience it, is better than living a life without it. I know Alfred Lord Tennyson said this better than me, but you need to hear the words. Listen to the point I'm trying to make with you. If you haven't screwed up too much with Bliss, don't. You two looked happy together and whether you believe me or not, you deserve happy. Everybody does."

"I know what you're saying is true. I just can't put that philosophy into practice. Every time I try, I stumble or fail, or my chest swells up like an over-inflated balloon. I just don't know what to do."

She held his gaze, pausing for a few seconds. "Keep on trying until you get it right."

Chapter Twelve

Bliss shouldered her small carry-on bag. A quick glance around the bedroom revealed no signs she'd been here. The stack of gifts had been distributed yesterday. All her work stuff was packed away in her bags and she was ready to head back to New York.

She made her way down the stairs. All she needed to do was pretend everything was fine for a few more minutes—just long enough to get out of the house so her parents wouldn't worry.

"Are you sure you need to leave today?" Her father waited for her at the bottom of the stairs.

"Yes, Dad. I have some things I need to take care of at work." She looked into the living room. Her mother was napping on the sofa. Keith was seated in the chair near the tree. He looked like the one needing comfort. "Mom is okay. I promise I'll come home again as soon as possible." She kissed his cheek.

"You seem unhappy," he said.

She tried harder to lift her lips. "I'm fine. Really, I am. I'm just a little worried that I might not get my report done on time."

"You're sure you're not upset about Marc. I thought he was a nice guy."

"Marc was great." Just saying the words tugged at her heart. "I couldn't have pulled off this holiday without him. Let's say he was a good distraction when I needed it. But, he had to get on with his life and I have to get back to New York and mine." She rubbed her father's arm, wanting to change this subject.

"All I can say, if he wasn't serious, why bother?" He shook his head.

She walked into the living room and kissed her mother on the forehead. With the help of her pain meds, she would probably be asleep for another hour. "Come on Keith. We better get going or we'll miss our train." She sighed. The only thing she wanted to do was get out of town, get rid of Keith, and curl up on her sofa, alone. There was a lesson to be learned somewhere in this mess. She needed to improve her sensors. Now she could clearly see Keith's shortcomings. He had always been selfish, but his good looks helped her overlook them. Marc was wounded. If she hadn't been so stuck on her infatuation with him, she would have seen his imperfection, too. She was drawn to men with issues. A weakness in her personality she needed to surmount.

The moment they stepped over the threshold, the cold air slapped her face. Her knees buckled. Keith draped his arm around her waist to steady her.

####

Just down the street from the Duncan house, Marc pulled into an empty spot and turned off the engine. The street was deserted. Wasn't the day after Christmas supposed to be filled with kids outside playing with the new sleds they'd received or trying to ride their brand new shining bicycles in the snow?

Bliss still refused to take his calls. She couldn't ignore him if he showed up at her door.

Lucy was right. He could spend the rest of his life hiding from his emotions or he could take a chance. Even if he and Bliss didn't end up married forever, they could have some fun.

His problem was he kept thinking about years in the future, when what he needed to do was think about right now. He'd taunted Bliss about worrying over her promotion or working so hard to impress her managers. But wasn't he doing the same thing? Instead of thinking about the moments they'd shared together, he had already rushed ahead to what would happen when she really looked at him and realized he was older.

Or what if she grew bored?

Or how could they have a relationship when she lived in New York and he lived in Delaware? He'd been so busy thinking about all the reasons they couldn't or shouldn't be together and not enough time thinking about how wonderful he felt with her.

The front door of the Duncan home opened before he could get out of the car. Bliss stepped out with Keith at her side. Keith's arm was wrapped around her waist and he was talking into her ear. From the privacy of his car, the gestured look intimate. Marc couldn't read her expression since her head was down, focused on the pavement.

He dropped his head. This kind of pain wasn't new. It was as if an old, angry friend had returned to ravage his life, again. But this time was different. As young as Bliss was, how could he have been so foolish to think she'd want to be with him. The waxing and waning of youthful relationships wasn't something he could handle. If this was what she wanted, at least he knew it now.

Bliss and Keith climbed into the waiting taxi and within minutes it disappeared around the corner.

Marc remained in the car. His toes grew numb. If he waited long enough maybe the feeling would consume his whole body. What had he expected to accomplish by coming here?

He turned the key in the ignition and pulled away. When he stopped in front of his house he was no closer to any answers. He climbed out of the car.

"Marc, wait up," Lucy yelled from her front door.

He stopped and pushed his hands deeper into his pocket, while Lucy tiptoed across a patch of ice in her slippers.

"I saw you leave this morning. Did you talk to Bliss—make up with her?"

"I went for coffee this morning, Lucy." He held up the cup. "Nothing more." He started toward his door but stopped midway. "Do me a favor. Please don't bring Bliss up again.

Chapter Thirteen

Marc stretched his legs out in front of him. His body was tighter than bark on a tree. Sitting in the darkened house for days, staring at photographs of him and Rachel that should have been put away years ago allowed Lucy's words to make worm-holes in his brain.

Christmas was over, two weeks removed. All the twinkling lights and plastic reindeer had been removed from the neighborhood lawns and life was getting back to normal. At least for some people.

He'd promised Rachel he would live again. Back then he had no idea how hard it was going to be. Packing away part of your life and starting a new one took more guts and grit than he had.

He wasn't in his twenties anymore. Rejection didn't mean he could go out and find someone else within days or that he had the stamina to even try. But one look around the gloomy room told him this was no way to live. Like a hermit crawling out of his hole for a few hours of activity before crawling back in and pretending he was normal. Once he'd been adventurous enough to take on a challenge, then Rachel died and he'd lost that courage. For a moment, outside of the Duncan home, he'd almost had it back—that feeling where he was willing to fight for what he wanted.

The sun filtered through the thin slits in the shutters. Another new day, but the same old fire burned in his belly. That fire was for Bliss and it wasn't going away. If he didn't at least try this once, then he never would and he wasn't worthy of her. Lucy was right—she always was—he needed to start living or he might as well have died with Rachel. He pushed off the sofa, grabbed his coat, and rushed out of the house.

He climbed out of the car in front of the Duncan house. From the sidewalk, he studied the house and took a deep breath before climbing the stairs and ringing the doorbell. He needed to talk to her. Explain stuff to her. If he gave his speech too much thought, he would turn back. The only thing Bliss could say was that she was no longer interested. If she did, he'd lay on some of his charm and hope he still had something of interest to her. But first, he needed to find out where she lived in New York.

"Hello, Mr. Duncan." Even though Bliss's father was only a few years older than him, to call him by his first name didn't seem appropriate.

"Hello, Marc." The wrinkle in the middle of her father's forehead deepened. "What can I do for you?"

"I know Bliss isn't here. I was hoping you could give me her address."

"Uh... Come on in." He stepped aside to allow Marc through the door.

In the living room, Bliss's mother was seated on the sofa with her foot propped on pillows. After shaking her hand, he glanced around the room. There was no sign that Bliss had ever been there. It was as if their fling had been erased from existence.

"I'd like to get in touch with Bliss. She's not taking my call."

"I wonder why that is." April Duncan cocked her head to one side. Her sarcasm wasn't hard to detect.

He'd been too busy acting like an ass. Nursing the hurt, feeding it with constant sadness. Where was the hole that was supposed to open up and suck him in?

Her father motioned for him to take the seat in the chair across from him. He rubbed his hands together. "What happened between you two? She looked pretty sad when she left here."

"I tried to call her. Several times."

"I knew something was wrong with her. The way she rushed out of here like her panties were on fire," her father said. "I don't know what to tell you, Marc. When she calls, I'll tell her you stopped by." Her father stood.

"Could you give me her address in New York? I go up several times a month to meet with my agent or editor. I'd like to drop by and see her."

The glance that passed between her mother and father was evident. They probably thought he was a stalker.

"Of course, we can't give you that without her permission. We'll talk to her to see what she says." Her father walked to the door. He opened it without any preamble. A pretty good indication that he wasn't pleased with Marc.

Chapter Fourteen

Bliss walked out of the office building. All she could think about while at her parents was getting back to New York. Getting back to work. Getting back to her life. Now she had what she thought she wanted. But the euphoria that was supposed to come, hadn't.

There was some satisfaction in her old routine. The pencil skirts, the heels, getting to her desk early, leaving late, and the endless reports between the endless meetings. These things kept her distracted during the day, but at night nothing held back the sadness.

She tightened her scarf around her neck, the wind cut through the fabric of her coat. She ducked her head into the warmth of her collar.

"Bliss, wait up."

She turned to see Keith running toward her.

"I saw a lawyer today," he said with a big exhale of air. She could see his breath.

"Good, Keith." She wanted to get home and get warm. Whatever happened with Keith now was none of her business.

"We're meeting with management in about an hour." He looked over his shoulder at the entrance. "I wanted to thank you. For the first time in months, I actually slept last night."

"I'm happy to hear that. I think you're doing the right thing."

"I'm sure you won't be impacted by any of this. My lawyer says it should be easy."

They stood in an awkward silence for several seconds. He stared at her. There was something more he wanted to say. She could tell by the way he shifted his feet.

"I've got to run, Keith. Good luck in there." She pecked him on the cheek before hurrying toward her subway entrance. No amount of sweet talk or apologies that would change the direction she was headed now. The only thing she needed was to do her job, do it well, and get the promotion. The year-end report had been submitted on time. Roger was pleased. That's all that mattered.

She found a seat and flopped into it. Tonight, it was a pint of ice cream and a romantic comedy with a happy ending. Someone deserved one.

Her phone rang and she removed it from her purse. Marc was calling again. That made ten calls in five days. When would he get the message that she didn't want to talk to him? He didn't need to explain anything to her. She was smart enough to understand what he was going to say. She didn't need to hear it then, and she didn't want to hear it now.

Marc was persistent. He called every day. At least twice a day. And each time, she stared at his number while her fingers itched to accept his call. Why were men so hard to understand? When she wanted Marc to call, he was cool and unconcerned. She was willing to bet he'd come to her Christmas Eve dinner to tell her he was ready to disappear.

The moment she tried to turn off her feelings, he lapped at her feet like an obedient dog. Even Keith was being considerate now that she was beyond him.

At her stop, she trudged up the subway stairs, anxious to get home. There was no reason to rush, but the solitude of her private space was the only thing that comforted her these days. Only three blocks to her second-floor walk-up, then she didn't have to pretend until tomorrow when she opened the door to the world again. She stopped several feet from the entrance to the building.

Marc was there.

Standing in front of her place as if his appearance was normal.

As if he was expected.

As if he'd been invited.

As if she were late for their date.

He strolled from one side of the building to the other, his gaze fixed on the ground. If only she could turn away, run in the opposite direction.

But she wouldn't, because she couldn't.

She closed her eyes for a moment, giving her stomach time to return to its normal place. This had to be a trick. He wasn't supposed to be here. The instructions she gave her father had been clear and concise. Do not share her information. Marc had shown her he wasn't ready to be in a relationship. At least not with her. She wouldn't be silly enough not to take his action as intended.

She put her nonchalant face in place—the one she'd used so many times before when relationships fell apart. Something she was too familiar with. For a couple of minutes, she could do almost anything. She was getting too good at becoming tough enough to handle being strung out and let down.

She advanced toward him. Her heels clicked against the cement with determination. "Marc, why are you here?"

He turned around to face her. "Bliss." Her name came out of his mouth like a song. For a moment he only stared at her as if he was as surprised to see her as she was to see him. "You look beautiful, as usual."

"You didn't answer my question."

He rubbed his ungloved hands together. "Can we go inside? I just want to talk to you."

She released an exasperated breath. If she weren't exhausted, she'd resist him. "Okay." She marched up the stairs. "There is nothing that needs to be said." She punched in the door code. "We had some holiday fun. Then we went our separate ways. No explanations required from either of us."

He followed her up the stairs to the second floor. Not bothering to interject himself into her tirade. A skill he'd learned while unceremoniously dumping women, no doubt.

Inside the warmth of her apartment, she removed her coat, scarf, gloves, and shoes without addressing him or inviting him to have a seat.

She draped herself on the sofa like a fifties leading lady. "Can you make this quick? I've got a busy evening planned." She was being cruel but there was nowhere else to deposit the hurt.

He sat across from her, without removing his coat. "First, I want to apologize. I won't try to justify my behavior, but you deserved better than I gave you. I'm sorry."

There was so much sincerity in his words, she struggled to remain hardened. She stood. "Apology accepted." At the door, she placed her hand on the knob.

"Wait, Bliss." He held up his hand. "I...I..." He looked down. "The details of what I was going through aren't important, but you are. I want to give us a chance. I realize that now."

"How did you find my place? My parents didn't give you the address."

"No, they didn't. I had to call in a lot of favors."

"Marc, thank you for coming here. For saying what you have." She kept her hand on the knob. No matter what he said, she wasn't going to give in. Not this time.

He rubbed his forehead. His posture pierced her heart. He was just another man who'd screwed up and wanted to apologize. This was as difficult for him to say as it was for her to hear. She thought she could forget him, but she was wrong. What started out as an infatuation had morphed into something more.

She returned to the sofa. There was no will to fight her feelings for him anymore. If she was ever going to take a chance, then Marc was the one to risk her future on. This was the moment she'd been afraid to hope for.

He rushed across the room and plopped beside her. Like a man starved for food and water, he wrapped his arms around her, claiming her mouth the way she imagined he would in every dream she'd had about him every night.

One Year Later

Marc placed his arm around Bliss's shoulder and pulled her out of the way of a woman wrangling two large suitcases. Penn Station two days before Christmas, anything should be expected. But there was no way this time last year he could have expected they'd come this far with their relationship.

"This way, baby. Our train is boarding on Thirteen West." He guided Bliss toward the forming line.

"We should have rented a car. I think driving to Wilmington could have been a lot less stressful."

"But then it wouldn't have been a reenactment." He kissed her on the mouth, a gesture so simple but so satisfying.

She inched forward. "Let's make sure we don't reenact everything."

"Oh, don't worry about that. There is no way I'm going to let go of you again. Now that I know you have a tendency to slip away." He tightened his hold on her arm.

"You should have told me what you were going through. I would have understood."

"I didn't even know I was going through something until you left me. But, we're well past that. The only thing I need to worry about now is your father. I don't think he likes me very much."

"That's not true. I saw the two of you at Thanksgiving, laughing like old buddies."

"Is it my age or do you think it's because of what happened last Christmas?"

"I think he's jealous. You don't look forty-one, your stomach is still flat, and you've got the most beautiful head of hair." She reached up and tousled his curls. "He's only ten years older, but he looks like he's got way more years on you. So try not to show off how fit you are while we're there. No one-handed push-ups."

His heart swelled. "Have I told you I love you today?"

"You did, but you can always say it again."

He'd come so close to losing Bliss. The thought still caused him to pause. Whatever veil had covered his eyes was gone. The ghost of Rachel was gone. She still lingered in his soul, but not with the heaviness of before. Now he could almost see Rachel smiling down on the two of them.

Bliss sat at the kitchen counter with her mother. As long as her mother could move around in her house on the holidays, she was happy. The smell of roasted turkey filled the air. This Christmas was different from the last one. This year Bliss almost believed in the magic of Christmas.

"My goal is to pass this tradition along to you one day." Her mother pressed out the last dinner roll.

"Mom, my hope is that you're around always and will always have the stamina to get us all together for the holidays."

"You and Marc seem like the perfect couple. Are you as happy together as you appear?"

"I am, Mom. We had a lot of stuff to work through, but we did." She knew she was gushing but she couldn't control it.

"Well, he must be committed. Moving to New York was quite a commitment."

She looked over her shoulder into the living room where Marc and her dad were huddled together. Whispering. "What does Dad want to talk to him about?"

"I have no idea."

"Why did I have to leave the room? He's not going to say anything ridiculous, is he? I should go tell him our relationship is fine. He doesn't need to go meddling."

Her mother stood. At the refrigerator, she pulled out a pitcher of sweet tea and filled two glasses. "I have no idea what your father wanted to say for sure. I was only guessing. You know he doesn't run all his opinions by me." After putting the rolls in the oven, her mother sat beside her.

"Have the two of you talked about getting married?"

Bliss hesitated. Marriage was another whole realm. If most girls couldn't wait to get married, the thought seldom entered her thoughts. Marriage was for people like her parents, people who wanted to settle down. Settling down some-time in the future, maybe. What she and Marc had was just perfect.

ABOUT THE AUTHOR

Jacki Kelly has written dozens of short stories and several books. She has as many crazy characters roaming around in her head as she done in her books. She loves hearing from her readers and chatting with them, so look for her Newsletter.

Connect with her online:

http://www.jackikelly.com

Twitter - @jackikellybooks

http://facebook.com/jackikellyauthor

If you enjoyed reading A Season For Bliss, please tell everyone you know and please post a review for other readers on your favorite reading forum.

BOOKBUB NOTIFICATION

Follow Jacki Kelly on BookBub to be notified about new books or discounts on earlier books. Just follow the link below:

https://goo.gl/rW2LbA